"I'm not suggesting we rush into marriage."

Though that would suit him. He watched her head jerk up, her gaze meshing with his. "Take your time. Consider the implications." When she did, she'd see he was right.

Slowly, she nodded, yet didn't look as comfortable as she had a few moments before.

But Theo had a plan to convince her. And it didn't include Isla working herself to the bone in London while he was in Athens. At any other time, he'd stay in England to persuade her but he was needed at home, and it was an obligation he couldn't ignore. His family needed him now more than ever.

"What you need is to rest like the doctor said and get your strength back. A break from work. Why not come to Greece with me?"

Her misty blue eyes widened and he hurried on before she could reject the idea out of hand. "We can discuss my proposal in detail and in the meantime, the holiday will do you good." He paused and widened his smile. "What do you say, Isla? Can I tempt you?"

Growing up near the beach, **Annie West** spent lots of time observing tall, burnished lifeguards—early research! Now she spends her days fantasizing about gorgeous men and their love lives. Annie has been a reader all her life. She also loves travel, long walks, good company and great food. You can contact her at annie@annie-west.com or via PO Box 1041, Warners Bay, NSW 2282, Australia.

Books by Annie West

Harlequin Presents

A Consequence Made in Greece
The Innocent's Protector in Paradise
One Night with Her Forgotten Husband
The Desert King Meets His Match
Reclaiming His Runaway Cinderella

Royal Scandals

Pregnant with His Majesty's Heir
Claiming His Virgin Princess

Visit the Author Profile page
at Harlequin.com for more titles.

Annie West

REUNITED BY THE GREEK'S BABY

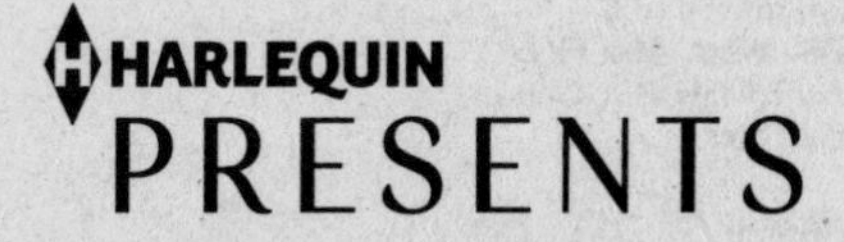

Recycling programs for this product may not exist in your area.

ISBN-13: 978-1-335-73910-0

Reunited by the Greek's Baby

For questions and comments about the quality of this book, please contact us at CustomerService@Harlequin.com.

Harlequin Enterprises ULC
22 Adelaide St. West, 41st Floor
Toronto, Ontario M5H 4E3, Canada
www.Harlequin.com

Printed in U.S.A.

REUNITED BY THE GREEK'S BABY

Dedicated with warm thanks to my reader friends,
Elizabeth M, Gill B, Jacqui L and Zeba S,
who were so welcoming on my recent
overseas trip.

PROLOGUE

ISLA SAT UPRIGHT in the hard chair, not meeting anybody's eyes. She'd known this would be difficult and had been prepared, but still the place made her shrink within herself.

It wasn't just the curious stares or unwelcoming atmosphere.

She huffed a silent laugh under her breath, tasting a hint of hysteria that she pushed down.

Prisons weren't supposed to be welcoming.

This, her third visit, should have been easier. Yet the cold institutional vibe, the grey walls and hard floors, the even harder stares of the staff and scent of heavy-duty disinfectant, got under her skin. And into her head, bringing memories of another place and time. The walls had been pale green, not grey, but the nose-scratching scent of cleanser and the throat-catching sense of desperation had been the same.

And the desolation.

Isla blinked at her hands, white-knuckled in her lap.

Then she lifted her chin and stared at the guard beside the door opposite until he looked away. It wasn't the past that unsettled her. It was the fact she wasn't wanted here.

For all they'd shared, all Theo had said and everything

she'd felt, he didn't *want* her now. Not her help or sympathy or presence. Twice he'd refused to see her. Today would make the third time.

She swallowed, a jagged lump blocking her throat as hurt consumed her.

Theo had more urgent things on his mind than their relationship, like proving his innocence and getting out of here. Being a foreigner, not able to speak more than a few phrases of Greek, she couldn't be much practical help.

Unlike his family and friends.

It was only when news of his arrest became public that Isla had discovered a side to Theo she'd known nothing about. That he was wealthy, well-connected and powerful.

Isla found it impossible to reconcile that Theo Karalis, the one making international headlines, with the passionate, endearing lover who'd swept her off her feet.

There'd been nothing endearing about his terse messages saying he didn't want her to visit.

'Ms Jacobs?'

She looked up to see a slim man in a dark suit standing before her. 'Yes?'

He sat beside her and lowered his voice. 'My name is Petro Skouras. I work for Mr Karalis.'

Isla's heart thumped. A smile cracked the corners of her tight mouth as relief rose. 'Yes?'

Her gaze darted towards the big metal door where the guard stood. Was she going to see Theo at last?

'He asked me to give you this.'

Petro Skouras held out an envelope. It felt flimsy in her hand as she tore it open. Isla read the note, for it was a note, not a letter, in two seconds.

Its meaning was clear but Mr Skouras was taking no

chances. His voice was kind but firm as he said, 'Mr Karalis asks that you don't visit again or try to contact him.'

He paused as if awaiting a response but Isla had no words. She scanned the note again, recognising Theo's bold handwriting. Not recognising the cold tone of command. This made it seem like they were strangers and she'd pestered him. Not as if they were in a relationship and shared a special bond.

Maybe they were strangers after all.

The back of her nose prickled as if tears threatened but it was an illusion. She was too shocked for tears. It felt as if everything she'd experienced in the last month, all the excitement and happiness, had been a dream.

'And I have this for you to sign.'

Isla stared at the typed paper he produced. It took a second for her blurry eyes to focus. When they did she gasped.

She'd heard about such things but never moved in circles where they were actually used. She read it again but the words didn't change. It was a non-disclosure agreement. If she signed she'd be barred from telling anyone she'd ever known Theo Karalis, or anything about him or their relationship.

Disbelief hardened into something stronger even than shock as each typewritten word carved itself into her brain.

Theo thought he needed a legal document to stop her blabbing about what they'd shared?

It was impossible. Unthinkable.

But the man she'd known had lied to her by omission about many things.

Obviously she'd been mistaken about so much. She'd

believed them soulmates. Yet he didn't understand her at all if he thought she'd sell her story to the press.

Isla took the fountain pen with a surprisingly steady hand and scribbled her name on the dotted line.

Petro Skouras's relief was obvious. 'Would you like me to see you to your hotel?'

'No.' She shot to her feet. 'I'm fine on my own.'

She had been before Theo burst like a bright ray of sunshine into her life. She would be again, given time.

Theo didn't want her. She didn't belong in his life. She'd just been a brief diversion.

Isla held her head high as she walked out into the Athenian afternoon, ignoring the pain in her breaking heart.

CHAPTER ONE

ISLA WRAPPED HER scarf around her neck then shoved her hands in her coat pockets as she walked down the street. Winter bit through her clothes. It was hard to believe that just four months ago she'd been…

Pain scythed through her chest. A reminder she didn't go there any more.

Dragging in a deep breath, she did what she always did when her mood dropped—focus on the positive. Find five things she felt good about. It was a diversion she'd learned as a child and it always helped.

Even if some days it was hard.

Some days it felt like a lie, but she always persevered and eventually, one day, things started to feel a little better.

Okay, five things. To make it easy she wouldn't look too far ahead. It was simpler to focus on the here and now.

One. The sun was shining after a week of English drizzle. The pale blue between the clouds surely invited optimism.

Two. Rebecca had promised chocolate brownies for morning tea, knowing they were Isla's favourite. Her almost empty stomach churned, making her frown, but then it settled and the moment passed.

Three. Rebecca. Her friend and boss was reason enough to feel grateful.

Four. The new wools might be in. It was always fun unpacking new stock, losing herself in the colours and textures as she restocked the shelves.

Five…

Isla caught the scent of cigarette smoke as she approached a man looking in a shop window. The acrid tang invaded her nostrils and her steps faltered as her sensitive stomach rebelled. He cast her a swift glance, lifted his phone to his ear and turned away to cross the street.

She took another breath, this time scented with wet pavement and the mint she'd automatically popped into her mouth. Thankfully her stomach settled.

Her gaze followed the man. Did she know him? His face, glimpsed in that quick, sideways glance, wasn't familiar. Yet something about the cut of his short, greying hair and nuggety frame rang a bell.

A shiver of disquiet rippled down her spine.

Isla hurried on. She'd cut it fine to open up on time. She couldn't dawdle. Yet as she approached the high street she couldn't banish a tickle of unease, the same feeling she'd had all week, triggered by a feeling someone was watching her.

When she reached the shop she shoved those thoughts aside. She was lucky to have this job and she intended to keep it.

She'd loved her studies and hadn't wanted to give them up but needs must. For now a steady income was more important than pursuing her passion for ancient history and her dream of becoming an archaeologist.

Isla's mouth twisted. Her track record with passions wasn't good. She'd only ever given in to passion with one man. A man who'd used then cruelly rejected her. There was a life lesson in there, but she refused to dwell on that now.

The morning sped by as she served customers, checked deliveries and dealt with online orders. The Friday morning knitting group in the back room finished and Isla got busy tidying up for Rebecca's afternoon patchwork class.

Neither she nor Rebecca had had time for morning tea and her stomach growled as she crawled under the large central table to pick up a stray ball of wool.

'Isla?'

'In here. I'm almost finished.'

She grabbed the grey eight ply and began to back out.

'There's someone to see you.'

That made Isla pause. None of her friends would drop in here during the day.

Plus something in Rebecca's tone jarred. Not disapproval. Caution? Isla frowned. Her boss was a friendly soul, not just welcoming to customers but genuinely warm-hearted. She wouldn't object to someone visiting her assistant.

Isla straightened and spun towards the door into the main shop.

Rebecca stood there wearing her velvet patchwork jacket, her grey plait over her shoulder. But instead of her usual smile, her expression was unreadable.

Isla moved closer. 'What is it? Is something wrong?'

Then she saw movement behind her boss. A tall figure moved into view, the shopfront windows in the main room backlighting him. For a moment he seemed more shadow than real, until he stepped into the doorway behind Rebecca.

Isla blinked as the shadow transformed into someone she knew.

Someone you thought you knew.

Isla's eyes widened, her hand clenching the wool like a lifeline.

She opened her mouth but whether to speak or drag in much-needed oxygen, she didn't know. A wave of clammy heat engulfed her and the table tilted as if lifting off the floor. Then the world disappeared.

'Isla. It's time to wake up.'

Rebecca's familiar voice filtered into the blankness, reassuring her. Something damp swiped her cheeks and forehead. The coolness felt good.

'Rebecca. Sorry, I…'

She what? Isla frowned, scrambling to remember what had happened.

She opened her eyes and there was Rebecca, her worried eyes belying her smile. 'There you are. You gave us a shock.'

Us?

Memory exploded and her skin prickled as if an army of ants swarmed there. Her eyes rounded and she turned her head. There was no one else in the room and the door was shut.

'He's in the shop, kicking his heels.' Rebecca watched that sink in, Isla's taut body easing back on the old couch near the wall. 'Not that he wanted to. He seems a man used to getting his own way. I had to threaten him with the police to get you privacy.'

'The police?' Isla stared.

'It wasn't necessary. But after seeing your reaction I wanted to be sure you wanted to see him.' Rebecca lifted a glass to Isla's lips. 'Here, you'll feel better with some water. Dehydration won't help. I should have insisted you stop for morning tea.'

Obediently Isla sipped. 'Rubbish. It's not your job to look after me. I'm a competent adult.' Though she felt like she'd been stuffed full of cotton wool.

She shuffled straighter, swinging her feet to the floor. For a second she felt light-headed but the sensation eased and she let out a relieved breath. 'I feel a lot better now.'

'I'm glad to hear it,' said a deep voice from the doorway.

Isla stiffened, knuckles whitening as she grabbed the velvet-covered couch.

That voice had an appalling impact. It conjured up memories of laughter and magic, moonlit nights by the sea. Of poignant happiness. She was sure that if she'd been standing her knees would have weakened at that deep cadence.

Rebecca, bless her, jumped up, expression militant. 'I must ask you to leave if you can't respect Isla's right to privacy.'

For a woman who barely reached five feet, Rebecca showed no qualms facing down the well-built man who topped her by almost a foot and a half.

Isla's heart swelled. How lucky she was to have such a friend. It was rare, having someone champion her. Orphaned as an infant, never adopted, she'd been alone all her life.

'It's okay.' Isla got to her feet, waiting to see how she felt. 'I'll deal with him.'

Rebecca looked from her to the man whose shoulders filled the doorway. 'I'll put the kettle on.'

'No need, Ms Burridge. I'll do that.' Behind him a bell sounded as the street door opened. 'You have a customer.'

Rebecca surveyed him coolly. Finally she turned to Isla. 'Call if you need me. I won't be far away.'

Isla nodded and turned to the kitchenette in the back corner.

'Sit down, Isla.' His voice came from so close she knew he stood right behind her. 'You need to rest.'

As if he cared about her!

Yet there it was again, sensation coursing from her nape down her spine, like a rolling wave of excitement. Or dismay.

Isla ignored it and flicked the switch on the kettle.

'What I *need* is a cup of tea.'

She turned to reach for some mugs but found herself looking at a firm chin and squared jaw. She blinked, taking in the flat line of a mouth that she knew in repose was carved in sensuous lines. When it curled into a grin it could make her heart stop.

Isla breathed deep, searching for calm. But that indrawn breath tugged in more than oxygen. With it came a subtle scent that reminded her of a seaside grove of pine trees and warm male flesh.

Something turned over inside but she told herself it was her restless stomach.

Yet she wasn't in a hurry to look higher. Her gaze lingered on his crisp white shirt and knotted tie of deep crimson silk, the cashmere coat across straight shoulders. So different to the jeans and short sleeved shirts he'd once worn.

This man oozed wealth and the assurance that went with it.

How had she never seen it before?

Because you had stars in your eyes.

Because you take people at face value.

Because you had no reason to believe he'd lie to you.

Isla stepped back abruptly, heart hammering.

'Fine.' Her voice came from far away but at least it was steady. 'I take milk. Rebecca has milk and one sugar.'

He didn't move. Just stood, waiting.

Inevitably, knowing it was unavoidable, Isla looked up.

Her breath backed up in her lungs. He looked every bit as gorgeous as before. The symmetry and strong planes of his face, the remarkable golden-brown eyes beneath dark brows, the hint of a cleft in one cheek that she knew deepened attractively when he smiled. The burnished olive skin. The dark hair that had flopped over his forehead, now cut short.

It was all familiar, evoking memories of intimacy and dreams, stupid dreams.

Isla clenched her fists against the impulse to reach out and trace those powerful, charismatic features.

'Hello, Isla.'

His voice had a rasping edge that she might, once, have associated with deep affection. Now she knew better.

She narrowed her eyes and that's when she noticed something unfamiliar. A scar near his left eye, ragged and still pink. Obviously recent.

Of course it was recent. It was four months since she'd seen him. The memory of that last morning before his trip to Athens, the laughter and tenderness, undid her.

Because it had been followed by rejection, all the more cruel for being totally unexpected.

Isla stumbled towards the couch, reaching for support. Instead of touching worn velvet her fingers met flesh.

Long fingers closed around hers and she felt the pressure of a warm palm at the small of her back.

'Don't. Touch. Me!'

Isla jerked away, flinging up her other arm to ward him off.

Over her raised hand she read his shock. Good. She'd hate to think she was the only one suffering.

Had he expected her to welcome him with open arms? She might have been naïve once but she'd had a fast-track lesson in reality.

Her knees gave way and she collapsed onto the sofa. 'The kettle's boiled.'

He looked like he was going to speak. Instead he turned away and busied himself with the tea.

It was bittersweet, watching him at such a domestic task, and it took her back to Greece. Except the man she'd known then wasn't this man. He'd been a mirage concocted to seduce a naïve foreigner into a brief romance.

The only thing real between them had been the incredible sexual compulsion that had led, on her side, to impossible fantasies. The affection, connection and understanding—those had been figments of her imagination.

Isla set her jaw and tried to survey him with a clear head. It wasn't just his clothes that had altered. He held himself differently, with rigid shoulders and a guarded expression.

He was uncomfortable? He deserved to be.

He swung around, gaze capturing hers, and she felt it like a blow to her heart. Those leonine eyes glowed molten gold, taking her straight back to the wonder of his lovemaking and the tender acceptance she'd felt in his arms.

Clearly it was a trick of the light.

She blinked. There, the impression was gone. His eyes were brown and unreadable.

'There are brownies.' Isla nodded to the biscuit tin.

He didn't move, just surveyed her in a way that made her feel scraped bare.

In the past she'd revelled in the fact he took his time to see her, understand her, make her feel unique and appreciated. Now she knew it was a clever seduction technique. He'd probably been seducing gullible women for years. It meant nothing.

She'd meant nothing. He'd told her so and backed it up with threats of legal action if she contacted him again.

Her heart dipped. She'd had a lifetime of feeling like an outsider. Theo's rejection had devastated her because she'd finally let down her defences. She'd believed in him, in *them*.

What was he doing here?

Whatever his motivations, this man was trouble. With a huff of feigned impatience she moved to the edge of the couch as if to get the tea herself but he forestalled her.

'Don't move.' He didn't raise his voice but there was no mistaking it as anything other than a command.

Deftly he assembled plates and mugs, poured tea and shared out the food. He put hers on the little table beside the couch, then with a stern look as if warning her from moving, he took a plate and mug through to Rebecca.

As soon as he left the room Isla leaned back, closing her eyes and suppressing a shudder of reaction. Being close to him again made her feel too much. She'd like to pretend it was simply surprise and anger but it was far more. The tell-tale pulse between her legs told its own story, as if her eager body still hadn't got the message that he was trouble.

Her mouth wobbled and she bit hard on her bottom lip, grappling with unresolved feelings she'd tried so hard to conquer.

When she opened her eyes, he was in the doorway but she pretended not to notice. Instead she sipped her tea, clasping the mug in her palms as if its heat could counteract the chill crackling her bones.

The door snicked shut and he strolled closer. With every step the air thickened, making it harder to breathe. She took another sip and wished she'd started with the brownie. Her stomach felt hollow but it was roiling so much she didn't want to test it by eating in front of him.

'When you've had that I'll take you to a doctor.'

'Sorry?'

Her head snapped up and she saw him, stance wide, cashmere coat thrust aside and hands shoved in his pockets, drawing the fabric of his trousers taut over powerful thighs.

'A doctor. You're as white as milk and you've lost weight.' He frowned, his gaze skimming her collarbone. 'You look gaunt.'

Isla clutched her tea close, her heart hammering so fast it couldn't be good for her. She wasn't ready for this. Had never expected to see him again, much less have him deign to talk with her.

'Thanks for your opinion. But I don't need a doctor. I'm perfectly healthy.'

His eyebrows rose. 'Fainting for no reason isn't a sign of good health.'

Deliberately she shrugged. 'I imagine no one reacts

well, coming face to face with the single worst mistake of their life.'

He stiffened, streaks of colour slashing those high cheekbones. But instead of retreating he moved closer. 'That doesn't explain the weight loss or the faint.'

Isla flattened her lips. She could tell him. She *should* tell him.

But her one attempt to contact him since returning to England had produced a threat of legal action. That rankled. Yet here he was on her turf, swaggering in as if he had a right to be here, demanding explanations.

Isla felt like she was on a seesaw, swinging wildly as the world tilted and turned upside down. 'Why are you here? Why the sudden concern?'

It couldn't be real.

Something flickered in those eyes and for a second she felt tremulous hope flare. The hope she thought she'd stamped out through the tough months since they'd parted.

'Simon is worried about you.' His words ground low as if dragged from his throat. 'He was stunned you'd rejected his offer of work next season and that you'd dropped out of university.'

Now Isla understood.

Simon was the Greek archaeologist who'd led the dig she'd worked on several months ago. The team, including students from her English university, had explored the remains of an ancient temple complex on a small Aegean island.

Once she'd have leapt at the chance to work there again, delighted that Simon wanted her back. She loved the work and hands-on archaeology was what she dreamed of doing.

But that career was over. Or at least on hold indefinitely.

'He couldn't believe it. He said you were one of the most promising students he's seen.' Once the praise would have delighted her. Now it reinforced all she'd lost. 'A colleague at your university told him you'd left suddenly with no explanation. They were worried you might be seriously ill.' Narrowed eyes surveyed her. 'I can see why.'

When Isla said nothing he went on. 'Simon knew I was coming to the UK on business and asked—'

'Asked you to check on me?' Isla's laugh sounded like a winter wind rushing through an empty corridor. Not surprising as inside she felt hollow and chilled.

Of course *Theo* hadn't been worried. He was acting for his friend. This was second-hand concern.

A sour tang filled Isla's mouth and she put down her barely touched tea. The irony. The man who'd threatened dire consequences should she approach him, checking her wellbeing.

Simon had introduced them one night when the team ate at a small taverna near the dig site. But she'd had no idea the pair were so close he'd ask Theo such a favour.

'Amazing. I can't imagine someone like you being close to someone as nice as Simon.'

His jaw clenched so hard he reminded her of a chiselled marble statue of a warrior, ready for battle.

Except this man's flesh was warm and hot, not cold marble. Her palms tingled at the phantom memory of his silky skin, tight over a body of hard-packed muscle and bone.

It was the final straw. She shot to her feet. 'You can tell Simon I'm fine. I want you to leave.'

She hadn't even finished speaking when he shook his head. 'Not without an explanation.'

A red mist descended, blurring the edges of the room. Vaguely Isla realised this was bad for her blood pressure, but the nerve of the man, pushing into her world and making demands…

Suddenly the energy Isla hadn't felt in weeks was running through her veins. She sparked with indignation and roaring fury. Disillusionment and despair melded with her lifelong sense of abandonment, the knowledge that she was always second best, never important enough to matter to anyone.

She should have known better than to believe she mattered to him, but she hadn't been able to resist building up hopes. She'd let herself believe and the disillusionment was crippling after having let down her guard.

All that hurt erupted in one lava-hot, volcanic burst.

'I don't owe you *anything*, Theo Karalis.' She spat the words so fast it was a wonder she didn't stumble over them. 'If you don't leave immediately I'll call the police and have you charged with harassment.' She drew a deep breath, holding his blazing stare, then spoke slowly so he heard every word. 'I have nothing to say to a murderer.'

CHAPTER TWO

LATE THAT AFTERNOON Theo stared through the gloom at the glowing window of the craft shop. Bright colours beckoned in a display that mimicked a cosy fireside nook.

But it wasn't really the shop he saw. It was Isla's uptilted chin and crossed arms, rejecting him and signalling her need for protection. From him!

Her glacial stare as she'd warned him off, calling him a murderer…

Outrage pounded through him.

She didn't mean it.

She couldn't.

She knew he wasn't a killer.

Yet he felt the slash to his gut as if she'd plunged a dagger into his belly. He'd assumed she still believed in his innocence. Understood he'd *never* hurt her.

He'd faced many things lately, more dangerous and life-changing than an ex-lover's disdain. Yet Isla's reaction hit him profoundly. She'd turned to ice before him whereas once her blue-grey eyes had danced with warmth when they were together.

Her reaction unnerved him. He, who'd survived a stint in one of Greece's toughest prisons. Who'd taken down one of the place's most feared thugs when the man tried to kill him, no doubt on orders from Theo's enemy, Spiro Stavroulis.

Stavroulis's hatred Theo could understand, even if it was misplaced. But Isla's reaction felt like personal betrayal.

There'd been no mistaking her scathing contempt. She'd looked like a stranger who believed the stories printed about him.

The press had taken Spiro's lead and crucified Theo's character, portraying him as reckless and violent, with a vendetta against Spiro's grandson Costa who they made out to be an innocent. The story was that Theo had deliberately pushed Costa to his death down a flight of stairs. They weren't interested in Theo's innocence. Or that Costa had been deplorable and dangerous. Theo knew that too well from the way Costa had hurt his ex-girlfriend Toula, Theo's stepsister.

A shudder racked him. This reminded him of those long nightmarish nights behind bars when he hadn't let himself sleep properly lest his cellmate try to claim the money Stavroulis had offered to anyone who seriously injured Theo. Or killed him.

Compounding his fear had been the prison rumour that Stavroulis had vowed to get at Theo by harming those closest to him. Desperate, Theo had organised the best possible security for his family. Fortunately *that* rumour at least hadn't been true. Stavroulis had standards and harming women was beyond them. But at the time it had spurred Theo to cut ties with Isla, keeping their connection secret so she wouldn't become a target.

Isla and he hadn't parted well so Theo hadn't expected a warm welcome. Nothing about that time had been as he would have chosen it but he'd needed to protect her.

She'd been so persistent, visiting the prison again and again, trying to see him. He'd taken that as proof that she believed him innocent. That had warmed him, despite knowing he couldn't maintain the relationship they'd begun.

Petro, his professionally distrustful lawyer, had suggested her persistence proved only that she'd discovered Theo was rich and stuck by him hoping for largesse.

Theo stifled a bitter laugh. Whatever she felt now it wasn't a desire for closeness.

Through the mayhem of his world disintegrating and the need to cut her loose, Isla's belief in him had given him hope. Especially when the justice system tried to grind him to dust, thanks to Stavroulis's powerful legal and political connections and his media outlets braying for Theo's blood.

Theo had deliberately pushed Isla away, yet her loyalty had been a glowing ember of brightness in a world turned to chaos. For the first time in his adult life he'd felt utterly, terrifyingly helpless.

Theo shoved the limo door open, unable to stand the enclosed space any longer. He told his driver to wait and stepped out. The damp air was better than being confined.

How long before he could stand being in a small space for any length of time?

Theo might be free and beginning to get his life on track but some things would always be different. His perspective on freedom. His gratitude for the simplest pleasures, like eating what he chose, when he chose. Making his own schedule.

But the taint of his arrest and his time locked away would linger until the true killer faced justice.

He raked his hand through his hair, torn between competing impulses. To clear his name fully and to protect the vulnerable. While he didn't *know* who was responsible, he feared it could be someone he cared for, definitely someone who'd been at the house that night. Put like that, his duty was obvious. He had broad shoulders. He was strong enough to weather the gossip and speculation.

The shop door opened and Theo stalked across, stopping a couple of metres away, not crowding her. 'Isla.'

She whipped round, eyes huge.

She couldn't really have thought he'd scurry away with his tail between his legs. 'I said I'd see you later.'

'I thought you were just saving face.'

Because she'd ordered him out? Because she'd threatened to call the police?

'I promised Simon I'd make sure you were all right.'

Theo guessed she'd react better to Simon's concern than to the news *he* was worried for her.

He'd been changed by the events of the last few months. But the alteration he saw in Isla scared him at a visceral level.

She was too pale, too thin. Her bright scarf and bulky winter coat couldn't hide her sharp cheekbones or the hollows in her cheeks, as if her flesh pulled too tight across her bones. He was alarmed at how fragile she'd become, her collarbone more pronounced and her pallor disturbing.

'I'm fine.'

'I don't believe you.'

Eyes bright and hard as diamonds held his. Despite the chill in her gaze, heat detonated in Theo's gut.

For months it had been almost a relief to know what they'd shared was over. It couldn't survive the mayhem that had engulfed him and he'd recoiled from the idea of Isla caught up in that. Yet some things weren't easily extinguished. No mistaking that fire for anything but desire.

Theo suppressed a bitter laugh at the way fate taunted him.

As if on cue the soft drizzle changed to stinging drops of ice.

Isla put up her umbrella. Theo turned up his coat collar but didn't move. A little water wouldn't budge him.

Remarkably he watched her determination waver as she saw the rain plaster his hair against his head and drips run down his neck. She'd always had a tender heart.

'Look, Isla.' He softened his voice, cajoling. 'This will be easier if you accept the inevitable and agree to talk.'

'The inevitable being you getting what you want? That's what you're used to.'

Her words were accusing. Their relationship had been entirely mutual yet she made it sound as if he'd taken advantage of her. The idea pulled him up short. Or was she referring to his wealth and the power that went with it?

Much good that had done when the police decided they wanted a quick arrest.

'I mean you no harm. You know I'd never hurt you.'

She said nothing and he felt the chasm between them as an ache in his chest, growing sharper with each silent second.

Theo had finally been exonerated but something stronger than pride made him blurt out, 'I didn't kill him.'

He couldn't bear it if she, of all people, believed him capable of such a thing. 'I'm not out on bail,' he continued. 'I'm free, all charges dropped. The authorities know I didn't do it.'

Even if the press hinted he got out of prison on a

technicality thanks to clever lawyers. There were stories circulating that he was guilty and that it would yet be proven. Spiro Stavroulis had lost his grandson and wouldn't rest until the culprit responsible faced the full force of the law. Meanwhile Theo was his scapegoat.

He wondered if the old man had even taken in the news that there was proof Theo was elsewhere on the estate when his grandson died, or whether grief blinded him to reason. Maybe Spiro thought that by pressuring Theo he'd move heaven and earth to uncover the identity of the one responsible.

Ice trickled down Theo's spine at the idea of someone else facing Stavroulis's hatred and all the prejudice he brought to bear, not just in the press but in the legal system.

Anyone weaker than Theo would crack under the pressure. Anyone whose resilience wasn't as strong as his… He had his suspicions about who might be responsible but hadn't been able to confirm them. He just hoped he was wrong.

'That may be so but I don't want to spend time with you, Theo.'

Isla's voice turned husky on his name, evoking memories of her crying his name as she climaxed in his arms. Of them sharing a joke, her voice breathless with laughter.

Of that last morning. He'd woken her at dawn and she'd surveyed him with sleepy eyes that reflected the light on the waves lapping outside the door. Her voice had been husky then too, with a tenderness he'd felt deep inside.

Regret sawed through him, like the swipe of a rusty blade against vulnerable flesh. Regret for how their golden idyll had ended. Regret for what could no longer be. And the pain he'd caused her.

But no matter how much she wished it, he couldn't walk away. He folded his arms, ignoring the weather, and waited.

Finally she nodded, her expression stern as if she already regretted her decision. 'Okay.'

'Excellent.' He gestured to the limo. 'We'll go to my hotel and talk.'

Isla retreated a step. 'Not there.'

Theo frowned. 'We can be private there. That's better than a café.'

Her shoulders rose and fell on a sigh. She glanced towards the shop where her colleague was closing up.

'All right. You can come to mine.'

Relief rushed through Theo. She *did* trust him. Isla wouldn't invite him into her home if she thought him a murderer. The idea of her believing him guilty had been an ache in his belly all day.

Yet his relief was short-lived, outweighed by concern. She looked fragile and unwell. He needed to find out what was wrong and what treatment she needed.

'We'll drive. It will be quicker and drier than walking four blocks in this weather.'

Abruptly Isla retreated under the shop awning. He followed.

'You know where I live?' Her eyes narrowed. 'Of course you do, like you knew how to find me at work. Did you have me followed?'

'Not followed. I paid an investigator to find you.'

'When?'

'This week. Why?'

Isla's expression hardened. 'All week I felt I was being

watched. Do you have any idea how frightening that is for a woman? I didn't know if I was imagining things or whether there really was someone keeping tabs on me.' Her chin jutted. 'A woman alone, going home in the dark…'

His belly cramped and Theo swore. He should have assigned one of his own staff to the job rather than hire a local. Someone would pay for this.

'I apologise. That wasn't my intention, far from it. But I take full responsibility. I wouldn't have scared you for the world.'

Silence beat between them, louder than the drumming rain on the awning above.

Finally she nodded but her expression didn't lighten.

It struck him that the change in Isla wasn't just physical. She'd been passionate about archaeology and with him, enthusiastic and giving. Their passion had made him forget his initial sense that she was a little more reserved than her colleagues. Not unfriendly, far from it, but cautious. And sexy, incredibly sexy. Now there was a gravity about her that he'd only seen tiny glimpses of before.

What had changed her? Was it all down to him?

Isla met that hooded stare and felt a rush of all those emotions she'd tried to lock away. Regret, longing, anger, despair.

And happiness. A sneaking burst of happiness that should be impossible but which shimmered in her blood like sunshine on water.

Even with his hair plastered to his head and his expression as dour as a thundercloud, Theo Karalis affected her as no other man did.

She'd told herself he hadn't meant it when he'd said

he'd see her after work. But part of her had known he'd be here.

He was no longer the light-hearted lover she'd fallen for. She'd always sensed a core of something solid in Theo, deep and strong. Maybe that was what had drawn her. That and the slow-dawning smile and superb body…

Now that fun-loving gloss had worn thin to reveal another man.

Not surprising given what he'd been through. For a second the impulse to touch him, to reassure herself that he was okay, overwhelmed her. But she overcame it.

He didn't want her sympathy. She should save that for herself. This was going to be tough.

Isla drew a slow breath. 'Shall we go?'

He gestured towards the dark car, its back door held open by a man she didn't know. 'After you.'

The trip was short and silent. Theo introduced her to his driver, a burly man with watchful eyes, then subsided into silence.

Isla had had all day to decide what she'd say if he appeared again and still she didn't know.

It was his fault. He'd rejected her in Athens and her one attempt to contact him since had made him threaten her with a charge of harassment. She'd given up thinking it possible to talk with Theo Karalis. If his dismissal weren't bad enough, trying to intimidate her with his power was worse.

Isla's mouth tightened as she led the way upstairs and unlocked her flat. She didn't look at him as she hung up her coat and took her umbrella to the bathroom to dry.

When she returned and saw him in her tiny sitting room her heart almost failed.

With the overhead light spilling over his dark, wet hair

she had a moment's terrible deja vu. To those glorious days in Greece, swimming in a secluded cove far from both locals and tourists. Theo always found the perfect places for picnics and making love.

Pain zigzagged through her, ripping the paper-thin defences she'd built so laboriously against Theo Karalis. She blinked in horror as her throat thickened and the back of her nose prickled.

She refused to think of those times. Better to remember the cold waiting room at the prison. Signing the paper that had shattered her last hope that he felt anything real for her. Then there was his threat to have her arrested.

'Here.' Her voice was brusque as she shoved a towel at him. 'I'll put the kettle on.'

Theo's hand skimmed hers as he took the towel and sensation shot up her arm, so powerful it verged on pain. It had to be pain. The alternative didn't bear thinking about.

Yet she couldn't prevent her gaze lingering over his impressive form. He'd taken off the cashmere coat to reveal a dark suit. But instead of looking like another city worker, Theo Karalis was in a league of his own. It was more than the superb tailoring of what she guessed was a bespoke suit. It was that tall, athletic body and the casual confidence of a man supremely comfortable in his own skin.

Once she'd found that incredibly attractive, the sense Theo had nothing to prove to anyone. She'd been drawn by his strength as much as his interest in her, so flatteringly intense.

Face it. You were blinded by his charisma and the way he looked at you as if no one else existed.

Now she knew his confidence was the arrogance of

an ultra-rich, privileged man, used to getting what he wanted. Including women foolish enough to be taken in by his charm.

Isla turned away, grateful for the routine of making tea. Theo's preferred tipple was Greek coffee, strong and aromatic, but she had none and she wouldn't apologise for that.

She kept her back to the living area, buying time. But she was aware of him moving about the room. Her nape tingled and she knew he watched her as he prowled the small space.

What did he think of her tiny flat with its second-hand furniture? It was quiet, clean and most importantly cheap.

It was bigger than the single room she'd rented near the dig in Greece but smaller than the old house she'd shared with Theo those last weeks.

Her pulse faltered, remembering. That place stood alone, around a rocky point from the village. It had felt like paradise with the aquamarine shallows outside the front door and the gnarled olive trees rising up the slope behind.

She'd fantasised about living there with him, not just during his holiday from work in Athens. That was before she'd found out who Theo Karalis really was.

'Tea's ready.'

Isla turned to find him just behind her, hair rumpled from where he'd towelled it, his jaw shadowed. He didn't look like the wealthy stranger who used limousines and wore coats worth more than she earned in several months.

He looked like Theo, her Theo, eyes glowing golden and beckoning…

She snagged a sharp breath and plonked a mug on

the table. It was so small that if they both sat their knees would touch and she'd be caught in his force field.

Isla took the ancient armchair. For a moment he stood as if debating something, then snagged the mug, crossed the room in three long paces and sat facing her.

'What is it, Isla? What's happened to you?'

She bit her lip, shocked at how sincere he sounded. Then, seeing his stare drop to her mouth, she lifted the mug and sipped her peppermint tea, pretending to savour its warmth. But inside she was all jitters.

Tell him. Tell him! It's what you tried to do after all.

Yet she hesitated. She couldn't ignore the way he'd treated her. 'You've changed your tune. In Athens you didn't want to have anything to do with me.'

Sombre eyes held hers. 'I'm sorry if I hurt you, Isla.'

If he'd hurt her! She blinked. Had she known him at all? It seemed not.

'It was for the best, but I realise it may not have felt like it.'

Too right it hadn't felt like it. True, there'd been no promises spoken between them but Isla could have sworn there'd been other sorts of promises made. Trust given and received.

Even if she'd got that wrong and the affection had been all on her side, he'd dumped her so brutally it hadn't just hurt. It had destroyed something she didn't think she could get back. The belief that she really *could* matter to someone. She'd grown up unloved and despite her positive self-talk, that belief had taken a lifetime, and Theo's concentrated attentions, to grow inside her.

Her chin notched up. 'I deserved better.'

Something flared in those leonine eyes. Then it was gone, his face unreadable. 'Yes, you did. I'm sorry.'

Isla sighed. Why rake over the past? He'd implied he'd acted for her sake but the plain truth was she hadn't mattered to him as he had to her. She didn't need to know more. She was simply delaying. Because she shied from telling this man the truth. If it had been the Theo she'd known on the island she wouldn't have hesitated. But this was a cold-eyed stranger, rich, powerful and moving in a social stratosphere that excluded ordinary people like her.

'I'm not sick.'

His dark eyebrows rose but he said nothing, as if the sheer power of his personality would force her to continue.

'And I haven't chucked in my studies. Just withdrawn for now.'

Isla's gaze dropped. Strictly that was true but there was no way she'd be able to return to university later. Even if she had time she wouldn't be able to afford it. Her mouth widened in a crooked smile. Maybe in a few decades.

'Why give up something you love? Something you're good at? Simon says you have a very promising career. It doesn't make sense.'

He paused and eventually Isla couldn't resist looking up at him. Heat trickled down her spine, vertebra by vertebra as she met his stare. How could she be so vulnerable to him after the cruel way he'd treated her?

He leaned forward, narrowing the space between them. 'You say you're not ill but you're clearly not well.'

Isla sighed, expelling the air in her lungs then dragging in a fortifying breath.

'I'm healthy. I'm just not able to eat a lot.' Another breath, another beat of her thundering heart. 'I'm pregnant.'

CHAPTER THREE

THEO COULDN'T TAKE the words in. He watched her watching him, waiting for his reaction, but his brain had seized up.

Isla, pregnant?

One reverberating thud and his heart started again, and with it his brain.

Isla, pregnant!

He couldn't stop his gaze sliding to her abdomen. Heat burned his skin and deep within his chest.

Isla, with another man?

Instant denial turned into revulsion, nausea searing his gut and making him grimace. It wasn't possible.

Of course it's possible. She's a passionate, attractive woman.

Yet Theo was having none of it. As if the sheer force of his willpower could make it untrue.

He breathed deep and slow, forcing himself to think.

It was sixteen weeks and four days since they parted. Theo knew precisely. In prison, counting the days since freedom had become habit. That had to be why he recalled precisely how long since he'd seen Isla.

Plus since then she'd spent at least a week in Athens,

trying to see him. Automatically Theo brushed aside the tangle of feelings that memory evoked.

His mind cleared and the terrible weight pressing on his chest eased. In that time would Isla have taken another lover?

He couldn't believe it.

Theo had been surprised by her sexual inexperience. He'd even wondered if she'd been a virgin the first time they had sex. If not, she'd been close to it, but he hadn't asked, not wanting to embarrass her since she hadn't referred to it.

Whatever her previous experience, Isla was an ardent lover. The memory of intimacy with her still had the power to undo him. Yet a woman didn't reach the age of twenty-four and be sexually inexperienced *and* promiscuous. He'd been honoured that she'd chosen to be with him. It wouldn't be in character for her to leave him and take another lover so soon.

Isla didn't let down her guard easily. When others from the dig partied to excess, she'd enjoyed herself but kept within limits. Despite her animation and warmth, Isla had an underlying reserve. Not coldness, but self-sufficiency. He sensed she participated on her own terms.

When she'd become his lover it hadn't only been sexual satisfaction he'd experienced. He'd felt privileged.

Now this. No other lover had ever caused more than a tiny ripple in the smooth waters of his life. Isla's news was a tsunami.

'You're having my baby?'

Any doubt disintegrated at her expression. Her eyes rounded as if he'd shocked her. There was something in her face too, as if she'd come to terms with something life-changing.

Theo knew that look. He'd seen it in the mirror often lately. 'Isla?'

'You accept my word for it?'

'If you say you're pregnant, I believe you. Why wouldn't I?'

'Not about the pregnancy. About it being yours.'

Her eyes that earlier had been a glacial grey turned misty blue. The same colour as when, a lifetime ago, she'd cuddled into him, breathless from sex and smiling dreamily as if he were some priceless treasure she'd unearthed on her excavation. The sight mesmerised him.

Theo shook his head. This was no time for reminiscence.

If today had taught him one thing it was that Isla was cured of that attraction. The knowledge was a lead weight in his gut, but he ignored it. He'd done what he had to do.

'The baby *is* mine.' It emerged as a statement. Definite, almost possessive.

That's how he felt. Possessive.

Of Isla.

And, as his gaze dropped again to her belly, of the child she carried. *His* child.

It would take time to absorb all the implications, but Theo felt no doubt about his feelings. His child. His responsibility.

His chest tightened on an upswing of emotion. Wonder. Excitement. Fear.

These feelings were so tremendous, he wondered briefly if his biological father had felt such exhilaration when he'd received similar news. But only for a second.

Of course he hadn't. There hadn't been a paternal bone in that man's body. To abandon the woman he'd got pregnant… Theo would *never* do that.

'But something's wrong.' Theo knew little about pregnancy but Isla looked nothing like the rosy-cheeked women he'd seen with their baby bumps. 'You say you're not ill…'

Which, frankly, he doubted. She looked wrung out, as if sheer determination kept her upright. It was all he could do not to pull her close, reassure himself that she couldn't be as fragile as she seemed.

Wouldn't that go down well?

'Tell me the truth. Is something wrong with the baby?' His throat thickened as if his body rejected the notion. He'd known about the child for just minutes yet he couldn't bear the thought of something happening to it. 'Aren't pregnant women supposed to glow?'

'Glow? I wish.' Isla's mouth twisted. Then, meeting his eyes, her expression changed, turning slightly less martial. 'Maybe I'll glow later. I've had severe morning sickness for too long to look the picture of health. But,' she hurried on, 'I'm assured the baby is absolutely fine. Once we get through this stage I'll put on weight.'

Relief seared through him that the baby was safe. Yet that wasn't enough. The sight of Isla worried him.

'Surely you shouldn't be so drained? If—'

Isla raised her palm, stopping his question. 'There's no need for a show of concern. It's unnecessary.' She paused. 'In fact, it's insulting. Don't play the worried ex.'

Her tone was cold. The way she said *ex*, like referring to something malodorous she'd picked up on the bottom of her shoe, made his hackles rise and his conscience sting.

Hadn't they been good together? More than good?

They'd been together only a short time, but he'd felt as if Isla had come to know him better than anyone outside his family. It had unnerved him even as he revelled in the way it intensified their every interaction.

'I *am* concerned.'

Surely that was obvious? She knew him well enough to understand that. Theo didn't lie.

'Really? That's very hard to believe. Especially as you threatened to have me arrested.'

Theo's head snapped back like he'd been slapped.

Logic had warned him not to come to England. He'd severed their liaison and it was a mistake to look back, no matter how tempting. Things were complicated enough without stirring the embers of a dead relationship. But he hadn't been able to resist and now found himself stepping off a precipice to somersault endlessly, reality turning on its head while he struggled to get his bearings.

'Sorry?'

Isla shook her head, eyes never leaving his. The scorn in them unfamiliar. 'Don't play the innocent, Theo. You know what I'm talking about. You threatened me.'

He leaned forward, hands on his splayed thighs. 'I've never threatened you. I never would.'

Her answer was a derisive snort as she lifted her mug.

'Isla?'

She didn't look up, as if her tea were more interesting than the father of the child she carried.

Theo's molars ground together. Indignation was a blistering rush of heat. Until recently he'd never imagined anyone would view him as anything other than a man of honour. Events in Athens had flayed his pride and now, unbelievably, Isla accused him…

'You need to explain. I deserve an answer.'

'*You* deserve? You *deserve*?'

Her eyes blazed, sharp as polished blades.

His skin pricked as if pierced. He'd never seen her so upset. He could understand ill feeling over how they'd parted. But not this.

'Yes, deserve. You're overwrought. You're not making sense.'

'Overwrought!' Liquid spilled from her mug as she slammed it down. Her face turned from pale to flushed. 'Next you'll tell me I imagined that letter.'

Theo paused. One of them had to stay calm. Briefly he wondered if her mood swing was bad for the baby. It couldn't be good for her. This was unlike the Isla he knew. He was both fascinated and horrified.

And reluctantly admiring.

In a perverse way her prickly aggressiveness appealed to a man used to fawning sycophants. But it was more than that. The glitter in her eyes, the sharp rise of her breasts as she tugged in air, her intense focus and vibrancy made him aware of her as a woman. A woman with whom he'd shared so many intimacies, such secret pleasure that even her concentrated fury was a reminder of the passion that had ensnared him.

What sort of man was he to be excited by a woman's fury? To prefer it to her steely attempts to blank out all emotion as if blocking him from her life?

He was like a kid taunting a pretty girl because any attention was better than none. Shocked at himself, Theo leaned back, away from her.

'I don't know about a letter. There's obviously some misunderstanding.'

'I suppose you don't know Petro Skouras either?'

'Petro? He's my lawyer.' One of them, and one of his

oldest friends. 'What has he to do with this?' Though Theo had a sinking feeling he began to understand.

'He wrote to me on your behalf. Said that if I tried to contact you again the police would arrest me.'

Theo's breath hissed. Horror prickled his scalp as he met Isla's needle-sharp stare.

How could Petro have done that to her? So many acquaintances and so-called friends had turned away from Theo when he was arrested. His reputation had been sullied with an avalanche of lies and innuendoes. But this woman had stood by him. Until he'd done what was needed and pushed her away.

It made Theo ashamed.

He swore softly and comprehensively.

He'd asked Petro to find a way to stop her visiting. Their relationship couldn't go on. At the time he'd feared old man Stavroulis might target her. Plus he'd needed to focus on fighting the case against him and dealing with the fallout. He had responsibilities that had to take priority over a budding relationship with a pretty Englishwoman.

Petro had suggested the non-disclosure agreement and Theo had reluctantly agreed. It was brutal and offensive but it meant she'd leave and he wouldn't have to worry about her as well as everything else in the fiasco his life had become.

'You're talking about the non-disclosure agreement?'

Her eyes narrowed. 'No, that was bad enough. As insults went it was pretty low. But I meant the threat of arrest for harassment.'

'Harassment? You?' Isla blinked as if his tone took her by surprise. 'When was this?'

Her throat worked. 'Does it really matter?'

'*When*, Isla?'

'When I was back in England. When I found I was pregnant.'

Gone was the strident fury, in its place a weariness that seemed to weigh her down. Her shoulders slumped and she sagged back in the ugly chair as if drained of energy.

Theo's heart hammered. He hated seeing her like this. He exhaled slowly, searching for calm. 'You tried to contact me?'

It was something he hadn't allowed himself to think about, but after doing what was needed and pushing her away, Theo had missed her. Missed the comfort of her on his side, ready to visit and support him. Ready to believe in him.

'I emailed your office. I'd tried calling but your phone number didn't work.'

'I got a new one.'

Because the press had got it and shared it. What use was a phone that rang nonstop twenty-four hours a day with abusive calls and texts? Some were from civic-minded citizens but he guessed most were from people paid by Spiro Stavroulis to make his life hell.

Theo pinched the bridge of his nose. He could imagine the situation. Petro being efficient and instructing staff to monitor personal messages. Had he red-flagged Isla's name?

Friend Petro might be, and well-intentioned, but tonight his ears would blister when Theo rang him to discuss the difference between help and unwanted interference.

'You sent an email and got a reply from Petro? He threatened to report you to the police for harassment?'

Dull eyes held his. She shrugged. 'Yes. An email with a letter as follow-up, in case I didn't understand the first time.'

Theo erupted from his seat, crossing the small room in three paces. Why hadn't Petro told him? Why take it upon himself?

The answer was simple. Petro was one of the few people who understood the full enormity of what he faced. Not only proving his innocence so charges would be dropped and he could be free. But protecting his family through the aftermath of that dreadful night in Athens, and again taking up the reins of a multibillion-dollar business that had suffered from the fallout.

Theo had come to London for one day only, all he could spare. He was needed in Greece as deals suddenly turned sour and negotiations stopped because people didn't want to deal with a company run by a social pariah. What hurt most was the way his previous good reputation and the company's name for excellence counted for so little.

He swung around to find Isla watching him. No wonder she'd been furious.

'I apologise. I didn't know.' He shoved his hands in his pockets, ignoring the urgent desire to take her hands in his. 'I had no idea you were treated that way, but I take full responsibility. Petro works for me. His actions reflect on me.'

Nothing had prepared Theo for the shock of being accused of murder. Yet the writhing feeling of discomfort and shame was stronger now as he took in Isla's drawn features.

What was she thinking? He couldn't read her. That

was another disturbing change. Once there'd been such affinity between them.

Theo cut off that line of thought. It was fruitless. He paced closer and her gaze tracked the movement.

'Do you believe me?'

'Maybe.' Her head tilted. Then finally, 'Yes.'

She didn't sound happy or relieved. Theo opened his mouth then snapped it shut. He couldn't expect her to welcome him with open arms.

'And you believe that I wasn't responsible for the death of Spiro Stavroulis's grandson?'

When she hesitated, something inside him died a little. His chest tightened. He'd weathered doubt and suspicion from the press, business colleagues and acquaintances. Yet this woman's doubt, the negation of her previous trust, affected him deeply.

'I can give you proof. A document from the prosecutor.'

Finally, when every taut muscle screamed at breaking point, Isla nodded. 'I believe you.' Then she ruined it by adding, 'After all, it's easy enough to check.'

Theo rocked back on his feet as if she'd punched him in the gut.

He stared down at her as if he'd never seen her before. Certainly she wasn't the woman he'd known.

Her rich, chestnut hair was pulled back in a low ponytail. His fingers twitched at the sense memory of those silky waves caressing his skin. Of burying his face in rosemary-scented hair. Her heart-shaped face was flushed yet still looked too delicate. As he watched she deliberately lifted it to look down her neat nose at him from eyes that gave nothing away. Her generous mouth was held tight and flat.

Didn't she *want* to believe him innocent?

For several heartbeats shock held him still. Then he realised what he was doing, brooding over how he was perceived when the most urgent issue was Isla's health.

He pulled out his phone.

'Who are you calling?'

'My assistant. It's not late. I'm sure with some persuasion we can see a top specialist here in London tonight.'

Isla was on her feet. 'There's no need. I *have* a doctor.'

'They're not doing a very good job.'

'Who do you think you are, coming here and making judgements?'

Theo stared down into those brilliant eyes, relieved to see that for now at least, Isla was sparkling with energy.

'I'm the father of the baby you're carrying.' He paused, watching her eyes widen. 'That's *our* baby. That gives me the right.'

His words reverberated into silence, penetrating deep, marking his very bones and burrowing into his soul.

He was going to be a father. *They* were going to be parents.

Theo felt a frisson of anxiety and wondered if he'd be up to that, especially given his biological father's appalling behaviour. But already his feelings about Isla and their baby proved him to be unlike the father he'd never known. At least he knew something about positive parenting from his beloved stepfather.

'This changes everything. You know that, don't you, Isla?'

'Of course. Why do you think I tried to contact you? But that doesn't give you the right to ride roughshod over me. I may be carrying *our* child…' Did her voice wobble on the word *our*? 'But it's *my* body and I make the decisions about my healthcare.'

'Ride roughshod?' He scowled. 'Because I try to get you the best medical care? You're exaggerating. You really think it's okay to be this exhausted, this sick? Are you absolutely sure that your condition isn't harming the baby?'

Isla said nothing but he almost heard her thoughts chasing each other. Her gaze shifted as if something beyond his shoulder suddenly took all her attention. Was she worried and putting on a brave face? It wasn't normal to be so unwell.

Theo shoved his hands deep into his pockets. 'I'm trying to do the right thing, Isla, to look after you both. Is that a crime?'

CHAPTER FOUR

THEO'S WORDS STILL echoed in Isla's head an hour later.

Doing the right thing. Is that such a crime?

Of course it wasn't a crime. In fact, the idea of getting a second opinion on her severe morning sickness was a relief. She'd been worried when it hadn't abated and she'd continued to feel so run-down and ill, despite the reassurances she'd received at her last check-up.

It was just the way Theo had taken charge without so much as a by your leave.

And that he spoke of doing the *right thing.*

Isla grimaced. Theo made it clear that he acted out of duty. Not worry because he cared for her in the way she'd once believed. His rejection had been brutal proof that what she'd believed a grand love affair had been, for him, a holiday diversion. When his life turned upside down he'd had no time for her, not even for her support. She simply didn't fit into his real life.

Now he was concerned to do the responsible thing. But his emotions weren't engaged.

Not with her at any rate. Yet, she recalled, there'd been one moment when he claimed the baby as his without question and a frisson of something powerful had trembled through her. He'd worn an expression she'd never seen before, one that made her heart roll over in her chest.

And she'd felt excluded.

Because in that instant it seemed that Theo's emotions *were* engaged. For the baby, not her.

Was that why she was so angry? Because she secretly craved Theo's attention?

The idea made a mockery of everything she'd told herself these last weeks about how she was better off without him. That it was a good thing she'd learned what he was really like now rather than later.

Not that there'd have been a later. She was sure their affair would have ended soon even without his arrest. It wasn't as if he'd fallen in love with her.

Isla bent her legs, tucking them up so she lay in a foetal position on the coverlet.

Determined, she yanked her thoughts in another direction. She'd had her whole life to get used to being on her own, never loved or wanted. Isla swallowed hard, ignoring the familiar hurt. Because it was an old truth, known since childhood, even if for a short time in Greece she'd forgotten.

Anyway, that was about to change. Her lips curved in a smile. There *would* be love. She had so much to give her child, and surely it would love her in return.

Believing in Theo might have been a mistake but this pregnancy felt like the most wonderful, miraculous thing in her life. Despite the sickness. Despite even the need to give up her dream of archaeology. Maybe one day she could go back to that. Isla deliberately ignored the pragmatic voice in her head that told her that wasn't going to be possible.

Had she imagined the flash of emotion on Theo's face

that made her think he really did care about the baby? What about earlier, when he'd first heard about the pregnancy? He'd frowned, his mouth drawing back in a grimace of disapproval. She hadn't imagined *that.*

Far from looking like a man excited by the prospect of a child, he'd looked like someone who'd received distasteful news. It had cut her to the heart. She'd taken it as confirmation of what she'd known, that he didn't want to have any more to do with her.

And yet…

Face it. You have no idea what's going on in his head. You never did. What you took for the beginnings of true love was just a vacation seduction.

Isla slid her hand over her flat abdomen, still stunned after all this time at the reality of her pregnancy. If it weren't for the sickness, it wouldn't seem real.

She stared at the bedroom curtains in swirling shades of blue. How often had she lain here, concentrating on that pattern as she fought down morning sickness?

But this time it was different. She heard a muffled noise from the other room and her heart lurched at just how different.

She wasn't resting because she was nauseous, though she did still feel a little light-headed. She was here because Theo insisted she rest before dinner arrived. The dinner he'd arranged so they could talk some more. And she, feeling hollowed out by the impact of one too many surprises, had finally agreed.

That still surprised her. She told herself it was because it had been a long day in a tough week in a difficult few months. It couldn't be because it was a relief, just once, to let someone else organise practicalities, like a meal she probably wouldn't be able to keep down.

Instead of being alone in her tiny flat, Theo was in the next room, so close her skin still tingled from the electric charge that had sparked between them.

A spark she'd told herself had been a figment of an overactive imagination.

He'd touched her and it had been like lightning dancing across her skin. Worse, she'd been shocked at how much she wanted more. Even his scent, of pines, sunshine and the sea, had threatened to undo her.

A knock sounded on the door.

'Wait!' She scrambled up, swinging her legs off the bed. She didn't want Theo in here. It was hard enough sometimes, trying to sleep with memories of the past tormenting her. She didn't need images of him here in her bedroom.

Theo had taken off his jacket when she emerged. That stopped her in the doorway, her heart tripping to a faster beat as she took in his broad-shouldered, narrow-hipped frame.

He had his back to her as he laid out food on her small table.

His sleeves were rolled up and those strong, sinewy forearms, dusted with dark hair, made her breath catch. Isla remembered the feel of his skin against hers, the surprisingly silky softness of that hair tickling her body and the heat his muscle-hardened frame exuded.

The deft, knowing touch of those capable hands as Theo explored her body and took her to places she'd never been before.

Setting her mouth, Isla told herself it was no wonder he'd haunted her thoughts and dreams. No other man had given her such experiences. One day they'd be memories to treasure, once she was over the heartbreak he'd created.

He turned and she saw his tie was gone, the top few buttons of his shirt open to reveal a V of golden skin. Deliberately she averted her gaze. He looked almost too masculine. Too strong and charismatic.

Their affair was over. Neither of them wanted to revive it. Theo because he'd never been serious about her and she because she needed to protect herself.

It's a little too late for that.

'Feel better?'

His gaze snared hers. She tried to read it and failed. What was new? She'd never really understood him, until it was too late.

'A little.'

Which surprised her. She'd been so wound up she hadn't thought she'd be able to relax with Theo Karalis prowling around her home.

She moved closer to the table, frowning. There were containers everywhere, not just on the table but filling all the counter space.

'What's all this?'

He shrugged and she looked away, not wanting to watch the play of his powerful muscles through the fine material of his shirt.

'Dinner. I didn't know what you felt like so I got a selection.' He paused. 'I know you like spicy food but I thought it might be better to avoid that with your morning sickness.'

Isla nodded and took a seat. 'Good idea. But you're right, I'm hungry.'

It surprised her. Her nausea wasn't confined to mornings and sometimes just the thought of preparing food, even cheese on toast, was almost too much. She only persevered because she knew the baby needed sustenance.

'Excellent.'

He flashed a spontaneous smile and for a moment she was transported back to that tiny dot of land in the Aegean that held one small village, an archaeological site, some olive and pistachio groves, and the secluded little house they'd shared for a short time. When life had seemed glorious with happiness and possibility. Because of Theo.

Heat suffused her, the warmth of wellbeing and excitement. But only for a second, until her brain kicked into gear and reality crashed down.

She scowled and looked away, reaching for a carafe of water and pouring a glass. From her peripheral vision she saw his face settle into stark lines.

Had he expected to win her over with a smile? Fat chance.

'Are you eating too?'

'When you've decided what you want.'

Like a waiter, he ran through the menu, lifting off lid after lid so the room filled with tantalising aromas. To her amazement, Isla found herself salivating. It all looked and smelled wonderful.

There were no local takeaway outlets that served food like this. Each dish looked exquisite. 'Where did this come from?'

Theo named a luxury hotel in central London, known the world over. The sort of place Isla would never even consider entering. Startled, she looked up to meet his unreadable stare. Was she supposed to be impressed that he'd spent so much? But then he was one of the richest men in Europe.

Her jaw clenched as she recalled how he'd kept that little fact from her in Greece.

Had he been afraid that if she found out she'd have expected expensive gifts? Or was it that he'd preferred to play a role, slumming it with the naïve foreign student for a few weeks before returning to his pampered, privileged life?

'I thought, with an upset stomach, you wouldn't appreciate a greasy takeaway. That's all that was on offer locally.'

His words cut through her bitter thoughts, and he was right. This food actually tempted her to eat. His thoughtfulness and the trouble he'd gone to surprised her. Until she remembered his words about doing the right thing. That he no doubt saw it as his duty to ensure the woman carrying his baby ate.

It wouldn't be a good look if she collapsed from malnutrition.

'What's so funny?'

Isla shook her head. 'Nothing.' She paused. 'Thank you. This was very kind of you.'

She caught him watching her but chose not to meet his eyes. Instead she scooped up some fragrant lemony chicken and a selection of glistening chargrilled vegetables. Only as she began to eat did he help himself to a rich casserole of beef and mushrooms.

Isla swallowed a mouthful then paused, waiting. The feast before her was like a sensual overload, all looking delicious, all smelling fantastic. But she'd learned to be cautious and see if her stomach rebelled.

'What's the matter? It's not to your taste?'

That sounded like genuine concern. 'No, it's lovely.' She swallowed another forkful.

The other kitchen chair creaked as Theo leaned back. 'Good, I'm glad.'

It was more than good, it was delicious. The tastiest thing she'd eaten in she couldn't remember how long. Her lips quirked in a rueful smile as she surveyed her emptying plate. Clearly there was something to be said for having a fortune to spend on meals you didn't feel like preparing yourself.

They ate in silence and Isla felt herself gradually relaxing with each slow mouthful. If she didn't look at the big, handsome man across from her, she could almost enjoy herself. The glorious food which for once she was able to keep down. The end of the day with no more chores to be done. The cosy sense of warmth and comfort.

She blinked and stiffened. No, it couldn't be that she felt that way because Theo was here in her home. Because, despite knowing he wasn't for her, part of her still longed for him.

The idea appalled her and she hurried into speech. 'I don't understand how you can accept this as your child so easily.'

Theo's cutlery clattered onto his plate. 'You don't? You'd prefer it if I accused you of lying?'

There was an edge to his voice, as if she'd annoyed him.

Isla finished chewing and swallowing before meeting his stare. Sure enough the gleam in his eyes showed he wasn't as sanguine as he'd appeared earlier.

'Of course not. But it seems so unlikely. Remember I know the type of man you are and the sort of world you live in.' Frowning, he opened his mouth as if to take issue and she hurried on. 'Don't forget your lawyer had me sign away my right to tell anyone that we knew each other. Not that that was a loss. It's a period in my life I definitely won't be sharing with anyone.'

'Isla, it was for the best. I was protecting you—'

'No!' She raised her hand. 'I'm not interested in explanations. It's over. Like our relationship.' She didn't need excuses. She knew where she stood. Had known when he refused to see her in prison.

'My point is you inhabit a world where it seems normal, maybe even reasonable, to threaten people into silence. That non-disclosure agreement I signed is an example. If you'd known me as well as you pretended, you'd have known there was no need for a legal document. That tells me something about the people you mix with and how you see yourself. You think you're so important that everyone is eager to take advantage of a connection to you.'

Theo's eyebrows scrunched together in almighty scowl and his jaw clenched in a hard line. He leaned back, arms crossed over his chest.

He looked powerful and forbidding, and to her horror, still appallingly attractive. What would it take to kill this weakness she harboured for him?

'As for threatening me with the charge of harassment—'

He put his hands on the edge of the table as he leaned towards her. 'I told you I didn't know about that.'

'It doesn't matter whether you did. The fact is that your lawyer thought it necessary, he thought it reasonable to take such drastic action without checking. Clearly he believed you'd approve. That tells me that you and he expect the worst from people.'

Isla lifted her chin, holding his glowing gaze, challenging him to disagree. Of course he didn't.

Finally he spoke, his voice soft. 'Don't forget I was in prison at the time. Things weren't exactly normal and people were spreading untrue stories about me.'

A tremor passed through her. Regret? Sympathy? She'd tried for so long to blank this man from her mind and her heart because she felt too much for him. At one time she'd been frantic with worry for him. Now, hearing that hard, almost blank tone as he talked about being locked up and slandered publicly, Isla couldn't help but feel sorry for all he'd gone through.

She looked from her hands, knotted in her lap, back to those remarkable eyes of dark amber flecked with gold. 'I'm sorry. It must have been a nightmare.'

His gaze softened, or did she imagine it? His mouth rucked up at one corner, driving a cleft down his cheek and making him look far, far too appealing.

'Thank you. It was…memorable. But it's over now.' He paused and she tried to read the expression lurking in his eyes. Surely not amusement? 'Go on, you were saying?'

Isla blinked. How had the scandal and the wrongful arrest affected him?

The lazy way he leaned back in his chair, the rueful half smile and the vaguely bored look on his face almost had her believing he'd shrugged off the horrific experience. But she knew it wasn't true. She might not know Theo Karalis as well as she'd once thought she did, but he couldn't fool her completely. This was a man masking strong emotion.

Isla felt the snap and sizzle of his repressed feelings, the iron hard clamp of control. It both reassured, because it reminded her of the man she'd fallen for, and scared her.

She took another sip of water. 'My point is that, since you expect people to try to take advantage of you, it's out of character for you to accept my word that this is your baby.'

His eyes darkened as they dropped to her hand, now resting protectively across her belly. Isla felt heat flood her cheeks but refused to tug her hand away. The issue here wasn't her but Theo.

'Surely you want a paternity test?'

It was the sort of thing that went with non-disclosure agreements, surely? Like prenuptial agreements and the other legalities the mega rich used to protect their wealth.

'You're saying you left Athens and took up with another man?'

'No!'

He was being deliberately obtuse. Isla was thankful he had no idea how totally unrealistic such an idea was. She couldn't imagine any man ever affecting her the way Theo had.

Wasn't that the saddest thing out of all this? Lots of women had their hearts broken. How many continued to hold a soft spot for the callous manipulator who'd dumped them?

'Then I don't see the problem.'

Isla narrowed her eyes and crossed her arms. It was a gesture of obstinacy, and of vulnerability, emphasising her too-slender frame and fragility.

Once again Theo felt a tremor deep beneath his carefully cultivated calm. As if with a simple gesture, she unsettled the sturdy foundations of his life.

No other woman did that to him. Just Isla. He hadn't realised at first and by the time he did he couldn't work out what to do about it. Except tell himself it was temporary. That it would fade once they went their separate ways.

But here they were face to face after months of separation and every accusation, every expression of hurt, felt like the rake of nails drawing blood.

Surely she shouldn't still have the power to affect him?

He wanted to explain why he'd pushed her away but it wasn't just about protecting her from the press or Stavroulis. He shrank from trying to put into words the terrible taint he felt from his prison experience and the way the world branded him guilty. Besides, the damage was done. He'd ensured she was safe, but at such a cost.

Once she'd left Greece his priority hadn't been her but getting free to support his mother and ensure Toula, who'd fallen apart the night of Costa's death, got the care she needed. And making sure the family company didn't fail.

'I need a simple answer to a simple question. Why don't you ask for a paternity test?'

Had Isla always been this obstinate? Why did she have to pursue this?

Because you treated her badly and she's no fool.

Theo exhaled. 'You want the truth? It's simple. I know you, Isla. You don't lie.'

Her eyes rounded and her tightly folded arms dropped. As if he were one of her precious pottery sherds or an ancient coin that had jumped up and started talking to her.

Finally she spoke. Her voice was so husky it grated across every nerve ending. 'You think you know me so well?'

Oh, he knew her all right. Almost from the start she'd felt unaccountably familiar to him, her attitudes, her reactions, even her humour. As if they were old friends.

Even in the early days when all he'd really understood was that lightning bolt of attraction, the sense of connection had been as real is it was surprising.

'You're the woman who noticed the waiter at the taverna had accidentally undercharged the dig team for dinner and went back to pay the difference out of her own money. The woman who, with a colleague, first discovered the ancient helmet which turned out to be the most exciting find of the season's dig. When everyone saw how significant it was and your colleague was too shy to claim some of the credit, you made sure she was acknowledged.'

Theo had been there that day and seen for himself. In fact, it looked to him as if Isla had first spotted the gleam of metal and moved away slightly so her companion could make the actual find. He'd discovered later that the other woman hadn't been particularly useful on the project earlier but the find had boosted her confidence and enthusiasm.

Isla shrugged, her chin rising. 'So? That's a little different to claiming to be pregnant by a billionaire. What's to say I'm not scheming to get my hands on your money? That's what your lawyer will think, isn't it?'

'It doesn't matter what Petro thinks.'

All that mattered was what Theo *knew*. Isla Jacobs was genuine and honest.

How many of his friends and acquaintances could he say that about? True, his closest friends had stuck by him but so many others had proven themselves less than friends and less than honest.

Was that why his belief in her felt unshakeable?

'Of course it's my baby. You didn't have time to start a new relationship.'

Strange how the thought of Isla intimate with another man sent his stomach into free fall.

Though logic told him that hadn't happened, he could picture it in his mind with devastating clarity. More easily than he could imagine Isla's slim body changing to accommodate his baby.

Theo accepted the pregnancy as fact but getting used to the idea of an actual baby, of himself as a father, would take a while. Though, if he really focused, perhaps he *could* imagine Isla's pregnancy. His lungs thickened on a short breath. His palms tickled, as he imagined holding her ripening body against his, her skin silky to the touch.

Isla picked up her fork and took another bite of her meal. Theo barely had time to register satisfaction that his plan to entice her with good food had worked, when she spoke.

'It's been months since we separated. I could have been with any number of men.'

It was sheer bravado, he knew, yet he didn't like it. Maybe that explained the harsh edge to his voice. 'You were a virgin before you met me. Weren't you, Isla?'

'You're making assumptions—'

'It was pretty obvious.'

Not in a bad way. Sex with Isla had been memorable every time. That first night, with her so sweet and ardent, so generous yet so surprised, would always live in his memory. Locked up in his cell, fighting not to lose hope, worried about what was happening to those he cared for, he'd revisited that precious memory again and again.

Theo met her eyes and watched a blush rise up her throat to her cheeks.

'You think you're such a fantastic lover you spoiled me for anyone else?'

Her tone was belligerent and her eyes flashed fire but he read hurt there too and instantly felt like a louse.

'Of course not.' Though some immature part of him would like to think so. 'But after waiting so long to have sex, and being so persistent about trying to see me in Athens…' Her blush turned fiery as if he'd accused her of stalking. 'It wouldn't be in character for you to take another lover so fast.'

She said nothing, just clapped her lips together and put her cutlery down.

He went on. 'We had sex a lot and there was that time when the condom split. Besides, if you really were trying to fit me up for money you wouldn't have let Petro's letter put you off. You'd have written back with your news. You'd have hired your own lawyer. Or fed a story to the press for some astronomical sum and hope I'd agree to settle.'

As he watched, the colour leached from her features, making him wish he'd shut up.

She shook her head. 'You really do live in a different world, don't you?'

Being with Isla again made him understand just how different.

Theo couldn't help regretting how their tentative truce had fractured. He shoved his chair back. 'Would you like a hot drink?'

For the longest time she said nothing. Was she about to demand he leave? Except instead of defiance or anger what he saw was exhaustion. Her shoulders sagged and she leaned forward, supporting her drooping head on her hand and an elbow on the table.

The change in her was so quick it stunned him. 'Isla, are you okay?'

'Sure. Just suddenly very weary.'

The ghost of a smile flitted across her lips but she was frowning. He guessed it was only determination that kept her from laying her head on the table and sleeping.

'Go and get ready for bed. I'll clear this up.'

Her head lifted. 'But we haven't…' She lifted one hand in a half-hearted gesture.

He'd been careful as they ate to avoid mentioning the future. It had been more important that she get a good meal inside her. Besides, there'd been something innately comfortable, almost satisfying, about sharing a quiet dinner with this woman.

Until, inevitably, it seemed, she'd challenged and argued, as if unable simply to accept his presence.

'Haven't talked about the child?'

Isla sat up at his words, her back ramrod straight, eyes narrow with suspicion. Or was that fear?

Theo digested that, a rusty, metallic taste filling his mouth. Isla, scared of him?

His life had changed dramatically recently. He'd experienced things he'd never expected. But not this. The idea of any woman scared of him was anathema.

'It's late, Isla.' Actually, it was quite early but clearly her body clock said otherwise. How had she managed working and caring for herself, when she had so little energy? Theo made his voice as reassuring as he could. 'We'll talk tomorrow. You're right, we have things to discuss.'

'Tomorrow?' She said it like a foreign, unfamiliar word. 'But you said this was a quick trip to London. I thought you were going back to Athens straightaway.'

'That was before I knew about our child.' The idea still made his pulse quicken. 'I've altered my schedule. I'll return tomorrow. We need to talk.'

CHAPTER FIVE

ISLA STARED IN the mirror, surprised to see colour in her cheeks for the first time in ages.

That's what a good night's sleep will do for you. And not waking to instant nausea.

She couldn't believe she'd slept so long and soundly after all that happened yesterday. It was as if her mind and body had shut down, unable to keep functioning and worrying.

That didn't stop her worrying now.

Whatever she thought of Theo Karalis, it seemed he wasn't a man to walk away from an unplanned pregnancy.

She rubbed her hands up her bare arms and shivered. The question being what *was* he going to do?

Her head whirled with possibilities. He lived a life of privilege and wealth. In a world where people could be made to sign gag orders to protect his privacy. Or threatened with legal action for trying to contact him. Would he aim to buy her silence? Provide financial support so they left him alone?

Or would he *want* their child? Would he demand regular access or even, her breath backed up in her lungs, demand to raise it? Try to buy her off or get sole custody?

Was that even possible?

Isla discovered she was gripping the edge of the bathroom basin with both hands, trembling with something alarmingly like the beginnings of panic.

Deliberately she grabbed her hairbrush and began to sort out her morning tangles, concentrating on long, rhythmic strokes and slow breaths.

She was letting her mind run away with her. Theo had lied to her and rejected her but he wasn't a monster.

He'd surprised her yesterday. He might have been prompted by duty rather than fondness, but he'd looked after her.

He'd sent her to get ready for bed while he tidied up and she'd been too drained to object. When she'd returned to the kitchen it was to find the food packaged up and Theo, sleeves rolled high, wiping down the table.

He'd looked at home, familiar in a way that made her heart squeeze. She'd drunk in the sight, memories of happier days filling her head.

Until he'd turned and seen her. True, she'd been wearing a tatty old dressing gown over her sleep shirt, but there'd been nothing in his expression, nothing at all, to hint that he found her attractive.

Once he hadn't been able to get enough of her. Or she him.

That blank, careful stare had confirmed what she already knew. He had no interest in her any more, except that she carried his baby.

He didn't desire her. That was over.

Isla tugged viciously at a knot till her eyes watered.

When the doorbell rang she reached for her dressing gown, to find she'd left it in the bedroom. The bell rang again, long and insistent. Enough to disturb her neighbours.

She hurried to the door, stopping to look through the

peephole. Her breath hissed. Annoyance, she told herself. It wasn't excitement. Not even a little bit.

Setting her mouth, she opened the door. 'Have you looked at the time? It's too early for visiting.'

Theo shrugged, that dimple appearing in his cheek and she silently chastised herself for noticing. He was closely shaved, hair slightly damp, and he looked disturbingly wonderful.

'Not too early for breakfast. You need to keep your strength up if you're going to work.'

He stepped through the open door, nudging it closed with his foot as he offered her a carton. In it were white bakery boxes, fresh fruit and takeaway cups.

The smell hit her, pungent and inescapable. Strong coffee, the rich aromatic sort that Greeks seemed to love. That she used to love.

Isla's insides rebelled, her nose crinkling in dismay as her stomach churned. She spun on her bare foot and raced for the bathroom.

Shocked, Theo stared as Isla ran, all long, gorgeous legs and rippling chestnut hair. Yet it wasn't surprise that tightened his grip on the box but a gut-slamming hit of need.

He'd felt it yesterday too, between the shock of Isla's news and being continually berated.

They weren't lovers any more. He'd had to end that for both their sakes. Going back again… He couldn't do that to either of them. Not with the mess his life still was.

But you want her, don't you? That hasn't changed. It wasn't just the news about the baby that kept you from sleep last night, was it?

The sound of the bathroom door slamming, followed

almost instantly by retching, set him into action. A few strides took him to the tiny kitchen where he left the food. Then he was at the bathroom door, debating whether to enter or give her privacy.

The sound of running water made him pause. How could he help? Unless she needed help standing, she wouldn't welcome him.

His intentions had been good. He'd been buoyed by her appetite last night, seeing her eat what looked like her first proper meal in months. But this morning… He shook his head. He should have thought. Morning sickness was called that for a reason.

By the time the bathroom door opened he'd dumped the box outside her apartment.

Her pallor was marked, the hair around her face damp. The change from the pink-cheeked, attractive woman who'd opened the door shocked him. He had to force himself not to ask if she were okay. He'd learned that with his stepsister, Toula, who was always prickly when she felt weak. Instead he held out the glass of water he'd poured.

'Thank you.'

Isla sipped it gingerly, not seeming to notice that spark of heat as their fingers touched.

One-track mind, Karalis. The woman's ill.

But he wasn't, which was why, despite his concern, he couldn't help noticing that in splashing her face, she'd also splashed her oversized T-shirt. It clung to her skin, lovingly shaping the upper slope of one breast.

Hastily Theo looked away, only to find his attention dropping to her bare legs. The T-shirt preserved her modesty, just, but he had perfect recall of the body now barely covered by thin cotton. Heat saturated him.

'Would you feel better sitting down?'

'Where's the coffee?'

'You want some?'

'Absolutely not!' She shuddered. 'The smell makes me nauseous.'

'In that case it's safe to sit in the kitchen. I took it outside. I wasn't sure what part of what I brought upset you.'

So much for congratulating himself that she'd been able to enjoy the food he'd brought. He'd undone all the good he'd achieved.

Good one, Karalis!

'Don't look so glum,' she said as she lowered herself slowly onto a kitchen chair. 'You weren't to know.'

But he could have guessed. It was logical that strong smells would disturb someone suffering from nausea. 'What can you have?'

'There are rice crackers in the biscuit tin.'

For the next five minutes Theo waited, leaning against the counter, watching as she nibbled slowly at a thin biscuit then stopped, frowning. After a long pause she took a careful sip of water. Then tried the biscuit again. Then another pause as if waiting to see if she could keep that down.

His mood darkened. If this was how Isla ate it was no wonder she was wasting away. Had last night just been a lucky coincidence? How did she manage to stay on her feet all day in the shop? Surely that drained her as much as the morning sickness?

By the time she was on her third cracker he'd had enough. He collected the food he'd put outside, leaving the cups.

Isla said nothing, just watched as he got out plates, one for the fruit and another for the pastries. The inviting scent of fresh baking filled his nostrils and he paused, shooting a look at Isla. She met his stare, raised her eyebrows and shrugged as if to say she didn't know how she'd react either.

It felt, for a second, as if time reeled back on itself, to those days in Greece when spoken conversation wasn't always necessary and they communicated without words. Their shared understanding had surprised Theo, as if they'd known each other years instead of mere weeks.

Whatever their apparent connection, those days were gone. He put the plates on the table and sat opposite Isla, watching for signs of returning nausea.

She seemed to wait too, as if unsure of her body's reaction. Then she reached for a plump grape and popped one into her mouth.

A smile lit her face. 'Yum. Thank you.'

Theo nodded but didn't speak. Something about her abrupt transformation, from wan and unsure to beaming, thickened his throat. Because she was grateful for such a small favour as fresh fruit? Because every day, every meal, it seemed, was a battle?

How long had it been this bad? Who had she had to help her?

He kept his queries to himself while she ate a few more grapes, watching her hesitate then reach out again. 'Raspberries! And they look freshly picked.'

Her gaze sought his as if wondering where he'd got such fresh produce out of season. Another reminder of their different worlds. For him money was no object. He guessed, his gaze scanning the small room, that for Isla, every penny mattered.

'Did you drop your degree because you're pregnant?' It was a crime, her not continuing. Simon said she was one of the best junior archaeologists he'd seen.

Isla's smile faded but she nodded. 'I couldn't study and have a baby. I needed to get a job.'

Theo's jaw tightened. He could support her while she finished her degree, but things weren't so simple. For a start, Isla would need other support, not just someone to pay her university fees.

That was assuming she'd let him pay. Her blistering animosity yesterday had left its mark. Theo guessed persuading her to let him help would be uphill work.

Just as well he wasn't easily deterred.

But for now her studies weren't the highest priority. 'I've arranged an appointment with an obstetrician today.'

Her chin lifted. 'Thank you. But I need notice to take time off. Rebecca relies on me.'

'Which is why I made it at lunchtime. I can drive you. I'll have you back in good time.'

Shimmering eyes held his and he sensed Isla sought for another objection. Because she didn't like him interfering? Because she didn't like *him*?

Theo's belly clenched in repudiation. But this wasn't about him. This was about getting Isla to do what was necessary to look after herself and their child.

Their child.

His thoughts slowed even as his pulse quickened.

'I'll talk with Rebecca. If the timing suits then I'll take the appointment.'

Theo nodded, forbearing from saying he'd already contacted her boss and cleared it with her. He didn't want any excuse for Isla to back out.

It had been a useful, if initially frosty, conversation. When the older woman saw he was serious in his concern for Isla she'd been remarkably helpful, even receptive to his other suggestions. But Isla wasn't ready to hear about those. Let her take one step at a time.

His ex-lover was strong-minded. He'd known it before but it was only now, as he saw how she battled valiantly with this daily struggle, that he realised how strong.

Inevitably his thoughts turned to Toula. His stepsister faced different problems, including years of early neglect and, he suspected, abuse. Was it any wonder she suffered with depression and had turned to substance abuse under the influence of Costa Stavroulis? Yet he couldn't help comparing Toula's attempts to avoid things she didn't want to face and Isla's determination to manage her life by confronting reality, not hiding from it.

Instantly he felt ashamed. That was unfair. Toula had demons even he didn't fully understand. She was doing the best she could and at least now she was getting professional help to deal with them.

'Theo? Did you hear me?'

'Sorry.' He found Isla watching him. Her eyes were brighter and she looked more like the woman he remembered. Her shining hair fell in waves below her shoulders, drawing his attention to her puckered nipples against the thin T shirt.

'Don't you want something to eat?'

Theo swallowed and made himself reach for a pastry. He was hungry, but not for baked goods.

But he couldn't sate his real appetite, for Isla Jacobs.

Apart from the fact she was unwell, this was no time to complicate things with sex.

He wasn't her favourite person after the way he'd pushed her away. Plus it would muddy the waters when they had important decisions to make. Theo intended to persuade her into seeing things his way. Ravishing her might bring short-term delight but at the risk of destroying his long-term plans.

Time to start implementing those plans.

He withdrew a folded paper from his jacket and pushed it across the table. 'I brought this for you. To confirm what I told you yesterday.'

Theo didn't want her having second thoughts about spending time with him.

Isla's brow furrowed as she read the official document. It was an English translation and confirmed that the murder charge had been dropped against him and he was a free man.

Theo knew she understood that or she wouldn't have let him into her home. Yet he remembered earlier yesterday, when she'd called him a murderer. He'd been astounded at how appalled he'd been. The world might insinuate such things but *her* accusation had wounded him in a way he hadn't expected.

'I'm sorry, Theo.' Her eyes were too big for her face as she met his gaze. 'I was being bitchy when I called you a murderer.' Her shoulders lifted as she drew a slow breath. 'I knew it wasn't true. I should never have said it. I was just…'

'You don't need to explain.' Neither had been at their best. 'We were both grappling with a lot. I just wanted to clear up any reservations.'

'I *am* sorry though. That you had to go through all that. It must've been terrifying.'

Theo sprawled back in his chair as if the memory of that time didn't still make him tense. 'It's over now.'

'Is it? Have they arrested the killer? I hadn't heard that.'

He sat straighter, no longer able to pretend to insouciance. 'No. Investigations are continuing. They're looking at everyone who attended the party.'

There had been a crowd at the Karalis family home that night. It would take the police ages to investigate them all, now their star suspect's alibi had been proven. Ice trickled down his spine as he considered how that investigation would affect his family. That someone close to him could be arrested.

'It definitely wasn't an accident? He didn't trip and fall down the stairs?'

How much easier if he had.

'Costa Stavroulis was in a foul mood. A witness heard him arguing with someone at the top of the stairs so he wasn't alone.' Theo's dislike of the man had been no secret, especially as he'd previously warned the guy away from Toula. 'Moments later he fell backwards. There were marks on his chest where someone had pushed him.'

The bruising proved he'd been shoved but couldn't provide solid evidence about the size of the person who did it.

Theo shook off thoughts of the crime and focused on Isla. She had to be his priority now. She and the child she carried.

'Why don't you finish your breakfast? When you're ready, I'll take you to work. Then you can check about taking time off to see the doctor.'

The morning went smoothly. More smoothly than any she could remember lately. Her nausea had abated soon after Theo's arrival and she'd kept down not merely some fruit, but a croissant and a cup of tea. Instead of feeling exhausted and empty, she actually had a little energy.

With the prospect of a lift in Theo's car, Isla had plenty

of time to shower and dress. Time to dither over what she'd wear. When she found herself debating between a warm, rust-coloured dress or jeans and a blue top that complemented her eyes, she was horrified.

She wasn't interested in impressing Theo.

Was she?

Firming her mouth, she grabbed plain black trousers. She reached for a pullover, but her fingers stalled as she touched the ultra-soft mohair Rebecca had let her take at an enormously discounted price. Isla had only finished knitting it last week into one of the nicest items of clothing she'd ever owned, a snuggly but stylish tunic in jade green.

She should shove it away. Wasn't the point that she *wasn't* dressing up for Theo?

Still she hesitated, then hauled it on and smoothed it over her hips. If wearing something nice made her feel more confident, there was nothing wrong with that.

Being with Theo was tough. He was the man she'd once imagined spending her life with. Now she wasn't sure if he was an ally or an adversary. Her nerves jangled. They still had to discuss plans for the baby. Then there was the obstetrician's appointment. Would it be good news?

When she got to the shop Rebecca had no objections to her scheduled appointment. Isla read relief in the older woman's eyes at the news she was getting another medical opinion.

It was after that when things started to run out of control.

The doctor confirmed that the pregnancy was well on track and discussed treatment for nausea. Fortunately she saw no reason for hospitalisation and after detailed questions, was hopeful Isla's symptoms might ease soon. Isla *did* feel a lot better than she had for ages, possibly because she'd had so much sleep and managed to keep down some food.

The doctor arranged a follow-up appointment but advised Isla to avoid stress and rest as much as possible. She strongly suggested time off work, to allow Isla a chance to regain some strength.

Isla's heart sank. That wasn't easy for a woman who needed to support herself and save for the future.

As if that weren't enough, instead of driving her straight back to the shop, Theo pulled up in front of a small, expensive restaurant, insisting she needed to eat before returning to work.

Isla sat in the luxury car, staring through the plate glass windows at the welcoming scene inside, and felt trapped. By the doctor's orders that she had no capacity to follow. By Theo's insistence that he knew what was best. By her body's weariness and the hollow feeling that said Theo was right and she needed to eat.

It was unreasonable to be annoyed, but she was. In twenty-four hours her world had turned on its head again and she no longer felt like she was running her own life.

It was too far to walk to the shop and she didn't have the energy to work out the bus route, yet she was tempted to get out and walk away. She'd been essentially alone all her life. Growing up in institutions she'd learned early to take responsibility for herself. The one time she'd begun to feel she belonged with someone had been with Theo and she'd been proved utterly wrong. Maybe she'd allowed herself to be deluded because she'd always secretly sought love.

Now the feeling she was no longer in control unnerved her.

'Shall we?' Theo reached for the car door, sure she'd agree to his plan. He hadn't even asked, just decided for her.

Isla drew a breath and ignored the urge to tell him she wasn't hungry. She needed to be sensible for the baby's sake. 'You go ahead. I need to ring Rebecca.'

He shot her an assessing look then nodded. But instead of entering the restaurant, he waited on the pavement, using his phone. Annoying Theo Karalis might be, but he respected her privacy. He'd left her alone during her medical examination too, only returning to hear the outcome.

Isla rang her boss and explained where she was. For some obscure reason she wished Rebecca would say the shop was busy and she was needed urgently.

'Of course you must take time for a proper meal. And it will give you and Theo time to talk.' Rebecca sounded enthusiastic. Probably because Isla had confided that Theo was her baby's father.

'Only if you're sure…'

'Absolutely! In fact,' Rebecca said, 'I've got someone coming to help this afternoon on a trial basis to see how she works out.'

Isla frowned. 'You're taking on new staff? Is there enough work for three of us?'

There was silence for a moment and when Rebecca spoke it sounded like she chose her words carefully. 'It's good to have backup. There have been days when you were so unwell you shouldn't have been in the store. I feel guilty about that.'

'You shouldn't! It's my job to be there. I'd never let you down.'

'I know you wouldn't, Isla. This is just a precaution. If this new person works out then she can fill in if I need to be away for a few days. And when the baby comes.'

Apprehension scuttled along Isla's spine like spidery fingers. She couldn't fault Rebecca's thinking. She *would* need more staff when Isla gave birth. But if this replacement proved good, and more reliable than a new mum managing on her own, maybe Rebecca would keep her full-time instead of Isla.

And maybe you're getting ahead of yourself.

She forced herself to smile as she spoke. 'It's good to be prepared. I hope she works out okay.'

'She sounded very capable. In fact, why don't you have the afternoon off? Then you can have a proper conversation with Theo. Oops. I've got to go. Enjoy your lunch.'

There it was again, the feeling that Isla's life was unravelling. Surely she was overreacting, yet that brief conversation compelled her to consider facts that previously she'd preferred not to dwell on.

She'd need time off work when the baby came. How long would her savings last? Rebecca was a good friend as well as her employer, but she had a business to run and couldn't leave a position open for her indefinitely.

Then there was childcare. Isla wasn't sure she could afford it and though Rebecca would probably allow her to take an infant into the shop, it wasn't a long-term solution.

And then there was Theo.

'Problems?'

He was at her door, an easy smile on his face but something in his eyes that wasn't at all easy. It struck her again that Theo was a very powerful man, used to getting his own way.

'Nothing I can't handle.'

She *would* handle it. All of it. Somehow she'd find a way to manage. She always had in the past and now she had her child to consider, all the more reason to be strong.

Ten minutes later they were seated in a luxurious booth as a waiter poured sparkling water and took their orders.

'Nice place,' Isla murmured as the waiter left. It was more upmarket than anywhere she'd ever eaten, with an air of understated elegance. Even the occasional clatter of cutlery and the murmur of voices was discreetly muffled.

'I'm told the food's good.'

'It should be, at those prices.'

Glowing brown eyes met hers and she saw a flicker of amusement. Almost like the old days—

Isla looked away. It wasn't the past that mattered, it was the future. 'We need to talk.'

'My thoughts exactly. We have a lot to discuss. Where shall we start?'

Isla turned back and there it was again, deep in those remarkable, leonine eyes. Determination. The look of a man who knew what he wanted and how to get it. Why did it unnerve her?

She sipped her water, feeling the bubbles hit the roof of her mouth. Like the effervescence in her blood when Theo had made love to her.

And wasn't *that* a memory best forgotten?

'Tell me straight, Theo. What do you want?'

His wry grin was far too appealing. 'Apart from lunch?'

'With the baby. You haven't said anything other than

to agree that it's yours.' Was it any wonder she was on tenterhooks? 'Do you want to be involved?'

Theo held her gaze as he nodded. 'Absolutely. I want our child to have the love and support of both parents. All the time.'

Isla blinked. What had she expected? That because he was a billionaire he'd hold aloof from their child?

'When it's old enough to travel we could sort out some arrangement.'

Her voice petered out at the thought of being parted from this baby she hadn't even met. It felt wrong. But she had to be reasonable. Theo was right, she'd do whatever it took to ensure her baby had the love and support of both parents. For she knew exactly how important that was, none better.

'You misunderstand me. That's not what I had in mind.'

'It's not?'

Theo shook his head, his eyes never leaving hers. 'I want our child to have both its parents. Together. As a family.' His mouth curled in one of those trademark smiles that, to her dismay, could still melt a vital part of her. 'I want you to marry me, Isla.'

CHAPTER SIX

THEO HAD NEVER imagined saying those words to any woman. So it was strange that they should settle, low and warm in his belly, feeling like truth.

He saw panic flare in Isla's expressive eyes but felt none himself. Prior to this he hadn't been ready to give up his freedom and tie himself to one woman for life. But he was ready now and when Theo made a commitment he stuck by it.

He'd seen the downside of broken families and wanted none of it for his child. The thought of abandoning a child knotted his belly. He'd *never* turn his back on this baby.

Yet it was more than that. There was something satisfying, almost reassuring, about claiming Isla for himself. Pushing her away had been incredibly difficult. A decision he'd regretted though he knew he had to do it.

Theo wasn't naïve enough to believe marrying Isla would be easy, despite the throb of sexual awareness that underscored every contact with her. In fact that complicated things. He needed to manage the situation and persuade her to his way of thinking. Instead he kept getting distracted by this enticing, infuriating woman.

Their physical attraction was one more thing to build on to convince her. Besides, they'd shared more than that, hadn't they? He hadn't imagined the joy or connection between them.

True, he hadn't told Isla the full truth of who he was, but that was because he'd felt he was sharing his essential self with her. The money, business connections and power weren't all there was to him. There'd been something precious in knowing Isla's response had nothing to do with his money. That she responded to Theo, the man, not the billionaire businessman.

'Marriage. That's a bit excessive, don't you think?'

Theo read amusement in Isla's face, as if she were too sophisticated to take the idea seriously. But she couldn't conceal the throbbing pulse at her throat or the way her hand shook as she reached for her glass.

Because she feared him? Everything within him rebelled at the idea and he forced himself to remember how she'd accepted his innocence. But if Isla wasn't afraid the stories of his guilt were true, what did she fear?

Maybe she's not afraid. Maybe she's decided she really doesn't like you.

Once, she'd *more* than liked him. She'd looked at him as if he'd hung the very stars in the sky and he hadn't been able to get enough of that, and her.

Pain was a black, aching chasm inside at what he'd lost. But even if she hated him now, she'd cared once. If her furtive looks proved anything, she was still attracted. That was a weakness he could exploit, for the sake of their baby.

'Not excessive at all. I've been thinking as I'm sure you have. I want our child to have the best start in life.' He shook his head. 'No, more than that, the best life it can have.'

'You think that's likely if it's raised by two people who don't care for each other?'

Theo surveyed Isla. Her chestnut hair was pulled back in a thick plait and she wore little, if any makeup. Yet that pared-back look emphasised her fine bone structure, the sweet curve of her pale pink lips, the intelligence in her eyes and the determination in the angle of her jaw. Her deep green top complemented her colouring and emphasised an innate air of elegance.

Familiar desire ignited, fiery trails heating his veins. How could the wanting be so sharp when she surveyed him so coolly? When she'd done nothing to entice him?

The first time Theo had seen her, Isla had worn dusty trousers, shirt and disreputable straw hat. He'd taken one look at her serious face as she discussed a fragment of pottery with Simon, then heard her chuckle, the sound like liquid sunshine, and hadn't noticed anyone else.

She'd captivated him though he hadn't been able to put a finger on why, exactly. She was more down-to-earth than his previous lovers. More self-sufficient. More earnest about her work. Yet when she gave herself, it was unstinting, opening her mind and body in a way that made him feel like he'd been given the world.

She was a woman whose beauty and personality transcended clothes. Yet the male in him hungered to see her in satin and lace, beckoning him to her bed.

'I care about you, Isla.'

No matter what he'd let her believe, what he'd told himself in prison, it had never been merely sex between them.

'You've got a strange way of showing it.' Her eyes flashed and it was like summer lightning stabbing out of a blue sky. 'You lied about who you were then you rejected me. That's not caring.'

Theo nodded and sat back as the waiter brought their food. He wasn't used to explaining his motives. In the years since he'd taken control of his father's company, he'd grown accustomed to making decisions, not just for himself but setting the direction for a commercial enterprise worth billions.

Perhaps that was why he felt unsettled. It couldn't be nerves at the idea Isla wouldn't accept his explanation or his plan to marry.

He waited till she'd begun to eat, wanting to make sure she *could* eat. But she tackled her food with no sign of nausea, as if she preferred to focus on that rather than him.

'You're right. I should have told you who I was from the start. I suppose I was used to being accepted as simply Theo when I came to the village. And Simon doesn't treat me any different because of the money.'

'But the money does make a difference when you're talking about billions.'

'True. Can you understand why it was appealing, connecting with a woman just as Theo? To be accepted for myself and not for status or material things?' He hadn't realised how important that was until he met Isla.

'You mean you're a poor little rich boy?'

Theo grunted with laughter. 'Hardly. I know how lucky I am to have all I do. And I have no trouble identifying people who are genuine and those who aren't. But it's a fact that people who meet me are aware of my wealth. It's not unusual for them to want to make my acquaintance because of what I can do for them. It's why my short breaks on the island feel precious, as if I'm reconnecting.'

Theo frowned. He hadn't thought about it in those terms before but it explained why increasingly he'd gravitated there and why he was considering building a house on the land where his great-grandparents had lived.

Athens didn't hold the appeal it once had, not surprising given recent disastrous events. On the island everyone knew who he was but treated him as an equal. They protected his privacy from outsiders, which was why the rest of the archaeological team hadn't known his identity.

'Reconnecting to what?'

He took his time, chewing a morsel of food while he collected his thoughts. What, indeed? He hadn't grown up on the tiny island where he and Isla had met.

'I wasn't born to money, you know.'

He saw her puzzled expression. She must be one of the few people who hadn't researched his life from the multitude of media reports. Theo didn't know whether to be pleased or disappointed.

'My mother was born on the island, in that little house where you and I stayed. She left to work in Athens before I was born. That's where she met my father and where I grew up.'

'It must have been a big change for her, from life on a tiny island to being the wife of such a wealthy man.'

'It was. More than you imagine.' Theo's smile felt tight. 'Constantin Karalis wasn't my biological father.'

It was clear from Isla's expression that she didn't know.

'My mother fell in love with a man who wasn't good enough for her. He dumped her when he discovered she was pregnant and she never saw him again. She spent the next ten years working every hour she could to support herself and me.'

'She didn't go home?'

Theo shook his head. 'Her father had very traditional views about children born outside marriage. I think she wronged him and hope he'd have welcomed her back. But she's stubborn too.'

'A family trait?'

He smiled. 'Could be. But we were happy together, we made a great team. I couldn't ask for a better mother. But believe me,' he leaned across the table towards the woman who carried his baby, 'I know how tough it can be raising a child on your own.'

She stiffened. 'You think I'm not up to it?'

'Not at all. I've never met a more determined, self-sufficient woman. If anyone could do it well, you could.'

Theo watched warm colour suffuse Isla's cheeks. It made her look flustered yet proud and beautiful and his heart plunged into a faster beat.

'But I don't subscribe to the theory that love alone is enough to raise a child successfully. Life is easier when each day isn't a financial struggle.'

'Are you saying that if I don't agree to marriage, you won't provide financial support for the baby?'

Her words stunned him. Instead of looking worried or outraged Isla's expression betrayed something like satisfaction, as if he'd proved her worst imaginings. Theo's patience frayed. He was tired of her expecting the worst, making him out to be some villain.

'I made mistakes, Isla, and I've apologised. But isn't your distrust getting out of hand?'

He shook his head, annoyed at letting it get to him. He was used to being the one people trusted. Whom they turned to for help. The one who solved problems and looked after his family. Isla scored his already battered pride.

'I meant exactly what I said, no more. My mother and I were happy but I remember days during the economic downturn when she lost her job and I went to bed hungry, even though she went without to provide for me. I remember her working for employers who took advantage of her, underpaying her and making her work long hours, but she didn't feel she could leave, because she needed the money for me. I remember how tough it was when I was sick and she couldn't afford babysitting but couldn't afford to take time off work.'

Theo paused, thinking of when they'd lost their apartment and been homeless for a while. Theo had been determined to keep them both safe, though being so young, he'd worried he mightn't be up to the task.

He recalled the gut-wrenching distress of those days. It was one of the reasons for his discreet support for subsidised housing schemes. No one should have to experience that.

'It wasn't just money. There were times when, I realise now, she would have loved a shoulder to lean on, to share the burden of bringing up a rambunctious boy, too full of energy. And times when I would have loved a male role model.'

His mother was amazing and he loved her dearly. Yet he understood in hindsight he'd missed what his friends had, a man to share with and learn from.

'I remember the day we met Constantin Karalis. We were walking a couple of kilometres to the bus and this big car pulled up beside us. The man in the back seat offered us a lift but my mother refused. She wasn't into charity and I think she was suspicious of accepting a favour from someone so obviously well-off.'

'She expected he'd want something in return?'

'Possibly.' He smiled. 'My mother is very attractive.'

'It must run in the family.'

To his surprise an answering smile tugged the corner of Isla's mouth. Had his revelation softened her view of him? It wasn't the vivid blaze of delight he recalled from the past, when her grins had been pure joy, yet even this muted smile felt like an incredible win.

'I suspect the same is true in your family.'

Her smile faded. 'I've no idea. I never knew my parents.'

Astonished, Theo stared. He remembered her saying she had no family and had deliberately not prodded for more information because her tone hadn't invited questions. He'd assumed they'd died recently.

'I'm sorry.' The words were inadequate. He couldn't imagine never knowing his mother or Constantin or even Toula. He felt devastated for what she'd missed. 'Who raised you?'

'Not family.' Her mouth compressed in a tight line that forestalled further questions. How could he not have known about this when in Greece he'd felt he'd known her so well? 'You haven't finished telling me about Constantin Karalis.'

She was trying to divert him. Curiosity seared. Theo wanted to know about Isla's past, not just because it might help him persuade her to his way of thinking but because he wanted to know *everything* about her.

The realisation was profound, another reminder of his powerful feelings for her in Greece. Before his world came undone and he'd made himself push her away.

With an effort he buried his curiosity, for now.

'Every day after that, the big car would stop before we got to the bus stop and he'd offer a lift. My mother kept refusing until the day it poured with rain and her umbrella blew inside out.' Theo laughed. She'd been so haughty and stiff when she accepted the ride, as if *she* were bestowing the favour.

'It was Constantin Karalis in the car?'

'It was. He was an incredibly patient man. It took a lot to win my mother over.'

'What exactly?'

Isla leaned closer, as if caught up in the story. Theo guessed she had no idea how engaged she looked. And how engaging. From the first there'd been something he couldn't name, something deep and true about her that reached out to him at a subliminal level.

A smile broke across his face as he sat back. 'He offered to take me fishing.'

She looked perplexed. 'Fishing?'

Theo nodded. 'At a place on the coast not far from where he lived.' He grinned. 'We had no luck, but it was marvellous. I didn't share my mother's reservations and the experience was new and exciting. Constantin treated me like an adult, not a kid.'

He paused, savouring the memory. 'The next time we fished, we had no better luck, but still it was fun. The third time, he persuaded my mother to let us take his boat out, as a treat for my tenth birthday. Later he confided he hadn't dared take me on his big cruiser earlier because my mother would assume he was trying to impress with his wealth.'

'He took you fishing to get close to your mother?'

Theo shrugged. 'We built up a rapport on those car

trips. But yes, he did. Before you label him as ruthless, using a child to get to its mother, you should know he and I remained friends for the rest of his life. Right up until he died we went fishing together and those times were some of the happiest of my life.'

Theo held Isla's gaze. 'I loved the man and he loved me. Until I met him fatherhood had negative connotations for me. The man who fathered me doesn't deserve the name. Being a father is about being there through thick and thin, the tough times as well as the good. About creating a warm, caring home.'

He watched her chest rise then lower on a huge sigh as if she only just understood how determined he was. 'You're telling me that's what you want to do?'

'Absolutely. The only things I have in common with my biological father are the genes I carry. I'm not going to turn my back on you or our child. I intend to be a proper father. Hopefully a good one.'

A spreading warmth filled Theo's chest.

Isla and he might not be in love but they were honest, decent people. They would care for their child and create a good home. The fierce physical attraction between them was a bonus even if at the moment, Isla seemed immune to him. That was something he could work on.

He looked forward to it.

'You look very smug. You're so sure I'll agree?' Isla pursed her lips. 'What if ours was a dysfunctional marriage? That would be no good for anyone, especially the baby.'

Theo kept his voice calm and low, as he did when reassuring Toula on one of her bad days. 'With goodwill on both sides there's no reason it would be dysfunctional.'

'You think you scared me with the tale of how tough

it was for your mother as a single parent? That I should marry you so I don't have to worry about making ends meet? Do you really think not having two parents who live together is the worst thing in the world?'

He watched the unconscious lift of Isla's chin. But in her expression was something more than accusation. Something that caught at his gut.

Fear.

A second later it was gone and she looked so calm Theo wondered if he'd imagined it. But her words echoed in his head, making him wonder anew about her upbringing. She'd had neither parent. Who had cared for her?

As for broken families, his own experience hadn't been bad, not like Toula's. Suffice to say he'd seen the terrible effect emotional scars from childhood could have.

'I'm not trying to scare you. I'm explaining how I feel. I believe our child will thrive in a united family. Far better than if we're shuttling him or her between us. Children seem to do best in a stable environment, don't you agree?'

Unwillingly it seemed to him, Isla nodded. 'Stability is important but that doesn't mean we have to marry and live together. Families take lots of forms.' She paused and Theo would have given much to know what was going through her mind. 'If we live separate lives it means we can both pursue our own…interests.'

Interests? Did she mean lovers?

A sour taste filled his mouth. The thought of Isla with another man was unpalatable. How civilised that sounded when at a deep, visceral level, something hard and primitive exploded at the idea. Theo had never been possessive but Isla was unlike any other lover.

She's the mother of your child. Of course you don't want her going off with anyone else.

Theo considered himself a civilised, reasonable man but, he discovered, he wouldn't stand for another man acting as father to his child. Surely that was at the root of his dismay, not simply the idea of Isla with someone else.

'What interests do you have that you can't pursue if we marry?' He kept his voice easy, concealing his harsh jangle of emotions. 'If you're talking about your career in archaeology, that would be easier if you married me.'

'Because you can pull strings to get me work?' Her tone was cool but her eyes shone brightly. 'I don't like nepotism.'

'Nor do I. I meant that if we were married, you'd have financial support to allow you to continue your studies and a family to help care for our child. You wouldn't have to manage on your own.'

For several seconds Isla said nothing and he wondered if he'd finally convinced her, until she said in a low voice, 'But at what personal cost?'

Theo stiffened. Was the prospect of marrying him so appalling? Despite his determination to woo her carefully, his patience frayed. Until logic overcame ego.

Why would Isla want you after the hurt you caused?

It didn't matter how noble his intentions had been, he'd lost her trust. That's what he had to build again. He needed to find out if she was just set against marrying him or against marriage in general.

The waiter cleared their starter plates, followed by another waiter bringing the main courses. Not that Theo was hungry, no matter how delicious the food. But the interruption gave him time to regroup.

After the staff had gone he took a bite of his meal, after seeing Isla start hers. Even then he waited. She'd barely touched her first course and he needed to be sure it was because of their conversation, not sickness. To his relief she ate slowly, but steadily.

Maybe because it's easier than arguing with you.

But Theo couldn't feel guilty about putting his case. It was for her benefit as much as the baby's. She'd see that once she had time to consider.

Meanwhile he needed to tread carefully. If she discovered the lengths he'd gone to in order to get his way on this, she'd dig her heels in even more. Not that he'd done anything wrong. Seeing a specialist had been a priority. As was ensuring she felt free to leave her home and her job.

Isla was loyal. The way she'd stuck by him when he'd been arrested proved that.

His out-of-hours conversation with Isla's employer had been carefully considered. He'd been frank about his concerns for Isla and his desire to look after her and the child. His worry that work and illness was affecting her health. Fortunately her employer shared his concerns, so when he spoke about taking Isla to Greece for a rest, Rebecca had been supportive, while reiterating that it was Isla's decision.

But Theo knew Isla wouldn't leave if she felt she was letting Rebecca down. So he'd had his staff busy finding be perfect replacement for her at the store and the woman was having a trial this afternoon.

Is that why Isla had looked bereft after talking with Rebecca? For a moment Theo felt guilty. But he wasn't forcing her hand, just ensuring there'd be no impediments when she agreed to his plan.

'You're not eating,' she said. 'Don't you like the food?'

Her concern surprised him. Did she care about him more than she admitted?

For the past twenty-four hours he'd seen a new Isla. That temper was new and though she'd been stubborn about visiting the prison, they'd never been at loggerheads before. Yet he saw both traits as signs of strength. They would have helped her through the last months. And, given her expression when her childhood was mentioned, possibly earlier.

'I've got a lot of my mind,' he murmured.

Her throaty chuckle surprised him. Heat trickled through his veins, pooling in his belly and reminding him of how this woman had once sated his mind and his body.

'Welcome to my world.'

Theo's mouth tugged into an answering smile. 'At least you've had time to get used to it. It still feels a bit unreal.'

It wasn't what he planned to say. Yet maybe it was the right thing to admit for Isla nodded, looking more relaxed than she had since they'd arrived.

She looked rueful, not upset. 'Tell me about it. It's a lot to take in.'

'Did you always want to have children?'

'One day in the future.' Her expression softened. 'I always thought it would be rather nice to have someone…'

Infuriatingly she didn't finish her sentence and he knew better than to badger her for an answer.

Someone what? Some partner to father her baby? Or was she talking about a child? Had she longed to be a mother? Had the people who'd raised her inspired her to want children?

Theo felt a wave of tenderness that had nothing to do with her pregnancy.

'I'm not suggesting we rush into marriage.' Though that would suit him. He watched her head jerk up, her gaze meshing with his. 'Take your time. Consider the implications.' When she did she'd see he was right.

Slowly she nodded yet she didn't look as comfortable as she had a few moments before.

But Theo had a plan to convince her. And it didn't include Isla working herself to the bone in London while he was in Athens. At any other time he'd stay in England to persuade her but he was needed at home, and it was an obligation he couldn't ignore. His family needed him now more than ever.

He leaned across and smiled encouragingly. He wasn't vain but he knew the effect that smile had on women, including Isla.

'What you need is to rest like the doctor said and get your strength back. A break from work. Why not come to Greece with me?'

Her misty blue eyes widened and he hurried on before she could reject the idea out of hand. 'We can discuss my proposal in detail and in the meantime the holiday will do you good.' He paused, making himself take his time so she didn't feel rushed or forced. Deliberately he widened his smile. 'What do you say, Isla? Can I tempt you?'

CHAPTER SEVEN

IT WAS A totally impossible idea, as Isla told Theo.

Going to Greece would be madness when she had no intention of marrying him. Even if the idea of having him remove her money worries was appealing. A billionaire's wife wouldn't have to worry about making ends meet.

But she couldn't raise his expectations.

Besides, she had a strong feeling that giving this man an inch would mean he'd take every future mile.

She understood now, as she hadn't before, what this child meant to Theo Karalis. When he'd spoken with scorn of his biological father, and the tough times he and his mother had endured, she'd seen a man with depth and passion. With strong feelings, not just about duty, which was what she'd imagined drove his need to be involved. Instead she discovered Theo already felt a bond with his unborn child.

He was determined to be a good father.

Isla was simultaneously nervous about the complications that would bring and delighted. Didn't her baby deserve love? Didn't it deserve everything good? All the things she'd never had.

Today she'd seen flashes of the man she'd known and fallen for so precipitately and it had set her battered heart yearning. Marriage would give their child the family she'd never had. Except theirs would be a sham marriage, not based on mutual love. Isla couldn't accept that. Better their child have two loving parents who lived apart.

Though she respected and admired Theo because of his feelings for their child, she now knew him for a powerful man used to having his wishes obeyed.

The idea made her shiver. Because he'd made it clear he wanted her baby.

Not Isla.

He wasn't interested in rekindling their romance, despite suggesting marriage. Far from it. He'd made no attempt to play on the intense attraction they'd shared. The attraction *she* still felt, despite every attempt to stifle it. He wasn't interested in her any more.

Isla was grateful he didn't pretend to feelings that didn't exist. Yet she felt disappointed. He wanted to marry her to get his hands on his child but not enough to try seducing her into compliance.

So how was it that now, this same evening, she found herself in a private jet about to land in Athens?

'Okay, Isla?'

She swung round to see Theo, beside her in another luxuriously padded chair, concern on his face.

'Why shouldn't I be?'

She'd been offered every luxury from heated, delicately scented face cloths to gourmet food and freshly squeezed juice. There'd even been a bed to lie on and a stack of magazines and newspapers, including two specialist archaeology journals that Theo must have ordered in especially.

His ability to make the impossible happen at short notice scared her.

Not for the first time Isla wondered at the coincidental timing of Rebecca finding the perfect substitute to take her place in the shop. And that the newcomer was available without notice. But surely Theo had had nothing to do with that. How could he? Her imagination was running rampant.

'Your jaw is clenched and I thought you might be feeling ill.'

He was right. She felt the ache at the back of her mouth and deliberately relaxed it. 'I'm fine. No nausea.'

In fact, apart from a moment when she got too close to someone smoking outside the airport, there'd been no queasiness since this morning. Maybe the doctor was right and her morning sickness *was* beginning to ease.

'But something's bothering you.'

Isla held his stare. 'It's been an eventful day. I can't help feeling I've been railroaded into this.'

Theo stilled then tilted his head as if intrigued. He looked curious but not in the least guilty. 'No one pressured you, Isla. I offered and you accepted.'

'I know. I'm sorry, that was unfair of me.'

She'd been uncharacteristically short-tempered since he arrived in London, caught in a welter of conflicting emotions that seesawed wildly. Was it pregnancy hormones making her suspicious and ready to anger? More likely the legacy of their past, when he'd let her down so badly.

What he said *was* true. This had been her choice. Yet it didn't feel that way. It felt as if the world conspired to make her fall in with his wishes.

Theo had suggested she fly with him tonight after taking a phone call during lunch. He'd looked at the number then apologised and excused himself. He'd returned looking sombre and saying he was needed urgently in Athens.

His observation that flying back with him would be easier than making her own way to Greece later was nothing but the truth. Flying privately was quicker and simpler than commercial travel. Plus he'd reassured her that he could have her back in London in time for her next doctor's appointment.

He'd even offered to pay her rent for the period she was away, since she wouldn't be earning. Before she could object, he'd added that she'd be doing him a favour in visiting Greece, allowing them to talk face to face and reach some decisions. The alternative was a series of long-distance calls, because the business crisis he had to deal with in Greece would take time to sort out.

Put like that, his suggestion seemed almost reasonable. Two mature adults determining how to raise their baby.

Still Isla had refused. She didn't like acting on the spur of the moment and she couldn't let Rebecca down.

But when he'd suggested she call her boss to ask about leave, Rebecca had been enthusiastic. Isla knew she'd been worried about her health, but not how much. Her boss had been adamant she take this break, overriding Isla's protests with assurances the replacement worker who'd done a trial that afternoon was excellent.

Isla had rung off feeling that Rebecca would shoo her out the door if she dared front up for work tomorrow.

Even then she might not have agreed, hating this feeling she was being herded in a direction she didn't want to go. Except who could resist the idea of a short break in Greece? Not to work but to rest and relax. Her weary body and even more exhausted brain couldn't withstand that temptation. She put it down to temporary insanity.

So here she was, looking out at the floodlit Parthenon below, the glittering blanket of city lights and beyond that the black velvet of the sea. A shiver kissed her skin. Excitement or warning?

'Maybe it's been too much of a rush.' Theo's voice sounded reflective as if he only just noticed how stressful today had been. 'You'll feel better in the morning. You can sleep in and spend the day relaxing.'

Isla would love to think so, but if she and Theo were under the same roof, she suspected it would be hard to relax. She squeezed her eyes shut.

What had she been thinking, coming here?

Panic welled. That was the problem. She hadn't been thinking, not clearly. It was madness to come here with Theo while her heart was still so bruised.

A warm hand covered hers on the armrest. A hand that was large and capable and shockingly familiar. Gently Theo squeezed and that too tugged the cord of memory in her soul.

'It will be okay, Isla.'

The velvet rumble of his voice caressed her and she swallowed convulsively, hating how badly she wanted to believe him. Was coming here one huge mistake?

'Of course. I'm just tired.'

She opened her eyes and summoned a bright smile that she guessed didn't fool him, for he frowned, the scar at his temple crinkling. He was concerned and every instinct told her he wasn't shamming.

Theo really was worried about her.

More likely worried about his child.

That shattered the moment of tender promise and just as well. Isla couldn't afford to be taken in by his plausible act of concern.

Earlier today he'd said he cared for her. Despite her hard-won defences, hope had shimmered brightly. For a moment she'd imagined his rejection had been a colossal mistake, until she realised she'd misunderstood.

He cared for her in a general, impersonal sense, as the vessel carrying his baby. He hadn't bothered to ask what she felt for him, whether she still cared for him.

His interest began and ended with the baby. His proposal wasn't about *them*. It was window dressing to cement access to the child.

Isla breathed through arrowing pain and drew her hand away.

Everywhere she turned that truth battered her. It was time she accepted it. She summoned another, brief smile. 'How long till we reach your place?'

Three weeks into Isla's stay in Theo's penthouse her hopes of guarding her heart against him were in tatters.

Instead of haranguing her about marriage he'd left her in peace, reiterating that she needed rest.

They ate breakfast together and when he returned from the office in the evenings, shared dinner in the smaller dining room. To Isla's surprise those meals were companionable, almost as if they'd re-established their lost camaraderie. Probably because they kept to uncontentious topics.

Given how Theo had opened up to her about his family, Isla found herself more in charity with him. Plus his obvious love for them tugged at her heart. It sounded like they were close.

Isla planted her hands on the balustrade of the apartment's landscaped roof terrace. But it wasn't the spectacular view of evening descending over Athens that she saw, it was the light in Theo's face as he talked about his parents.

She bit her lip. What must that feel like? She'd been drawn to him then, as strongly as in the days when she'd thought he was falling in love with her too.

She sighed. Was she still so needy? Just because she'd never had parents. She'd always dreamed of belonging, not out of a conscious act of charity but because she mattered. Because she was loved.

But you're going to have a child.

A bubble of excitement rose. For the first time in her life she'd have someone to love, who'd love her back.

She clung to the railing. The thought rocked her back on her feet, making her feel physically weak for the first time since arriving in Greece.

Every day her stress levels and tiredness were easing. Even her nausea abated.

Maybe the baby likes being in Greece.

Isla scotched that thought. Her physical improvement was more likely because she was ending the morning sickness stage and she'd done nothing but rest. A housekeeper produced gourmet meals and wouldn't let Isla lift a finger, not even make her bed. The shock on the woman's face the first morning when she'd found Isla tidying the bed had been priceless. And had led to Theo stressing again the doctor's orders that she rest.

Now she felt more energised. And more aware of Theo than ever. His smile made her stomach flip. The way he held back from pushing her about his proposal made her think maybe he *did* care, though not in the way she'd once hoped.

On those rare occasions when his hand brushed

hers—for he usually kept his distance—Isla felt a tremor through her whole body.

Just thinking about it made her quiver.

'You're cold.' The deep voice came from behind her and sure enough, there it was, that tiny, delicious shudder of recognition. 'What are you doing here without a jacket?'

Isla drew a slow breath, schooling her features so as not to betray the needy woman she became in unguarded moments. His concern added to the illusion of tenderness.

'It's far warmer than London in early spring and the sun shines more.'

She was turning when heat enveloped her. The warmth of his silk-lined suit jacket, imbued with that indefinable seaside pine scent that made her nostrils flare and longing pierce her.

For a second Isla indulged herself, imagining it wasn't his jacket enveloping her but loving arms.

Horror rose. How could she let her guard down like that?

She swung around, shoring up her defences, only to discover in his stern face an expression that made her soften. Isla revelled in it, her heart rising to her throat.

Until she understood what she was doing. Beginning to fall for this man all over again. She reached up to dislodge the jacket.

Adrenaline shot through Theo's blood as he saw Isla's face wearing that dreamy look, the one that had undone him so often.

His heart jolted with an emotion that had nothing to do with her pregnancy. But before he could identify it her expression blanked and she reached up to push his jacket off.

'Don't!' His hand closed on hers. They stilled, gazes locked. Did Isla feel it? The thundering pulse? The coiling, weighted sensation in the groin? The yearning?

Abruptly he stepped out of reach. But his palm tingled from the contact and his breath trapped in his lungs, swelling against his ribs.

'Leave it, Isla.'

She looked like she was going to object then thought better of it. Silence expanded as they stared at each other, a silence filled with his thudding pulse.

One touch had done that. One look.

Such power this woman had. It was unprecedented.

Because there'd been no one since her? Could it be that simple?

He couldn't trust himself to maintain the façade of disinterested concern if he got too close. It had taken all his resolution to leave her behind each day and head for the office even though he was wrangling several crises as other companies thought twice about doing business with him and hungry competitors snapped at his heels. Any thought that being freed from prison would end the nightmare had died as Stavroulis's continuing media hate campaign affected confidence in the company.

Theo was on a knife edge, juggling his concerns about Isla and the baby, his family and the company.

Yet it wasn't the company or his family keeping him awake.

Every night Isla was under his roof sleep eluded Theo. Each morning she looked a little better, a little brighter and he'd been thankful, though he functioned on a bare couple of hours a night.

Every night since she'd arrived, he'd spent hours in the study, working. Or in his home gym. Or in the private rooftop pool, doing laps. The pool had solar heating so even on a wintry night it was inviting. Yesterday he'd turned that heating off, preferring to take an icy dip in hopes of killing libidinous thoughts.

It had worked only until he fell, exhausted, into bed. Then he'd been consumed by memories of them together, moving as one, scaling peaks of fulfilment that surely his imagination exaggerated.

She took a step towards him then paused, frowning. 'You must be cold. You're only wearing a shirt.'

She was worried about him?

'I'm fine.' He was immune to the cold, given the heat searing through his veins at being close to her. He paused, trying to get his brain to focus on something other than sweeping Isla into his arms then into his bed.

'Do you want to go out for dinner?' he said abruptly. 'It would make a change from eating in the apartment.'

It was a spur of the moment idea but tonight Theo didn't trust himself to play nice and keep his distance. Not through an intimate evening alone, just metres from his bed and any number of inviting sofas.

Hell, even the dining table was a danger zone.

'I'd like that,' she said eventually.

Theo tried to read her. But it was no use, she'd retreated behind those walls she erected. He'd give a lot to know what she was thinking.

He had to find a way to get through to her. For their child's sake. And his own.

CHAPTER EIGHT

ISLA ASSUMED HE'D take her to a sophisticated restaurant. Instead the car had wound through increasingly narrow streets until he parked below the towering Acropolis and they walked through tiny lanes. On a summer's day it would be a tourist mecca but on this crisp night it was quiet.

She didn't notice a sign, just lights over the door, then they plunged into a cosy room with small tables, wooden chairs and checked oilcloth tablecloths. The place smelled delicious. Candles in old bottles flickered as they entered but other diners paid them little heed.

Not so the proprietor who hastened across, greeting Theo like a long-lost brother.

Isla knew some basic Greek but had no hope of understanding the machine-gun rapid enthusiasm of their host as he ushered them to a corner table. As they sat Theo introduced her as his friend from England. The owner, Georgio, welcomed her warmly before leaning close and assuring her that Theo was a good man. A very good man, he reiterated, and she was to pay no attention to the lies spread about him.

'It's okay, Georgio. Isla knows me.'

The man smiled and nodded, heading off with promises of food.

'No menus?' Isla queried.

Theo shrugged and grinned and she couldn't help but stare. He was an uncommonly attractive man, but that rare, carefree smile…

'It's easier to let Georgio choose. He knows what's best each day and he never disappoints.'

'You know him well? Obviously he thinks a lot of you.'

'We go back a while.'

He didn't elaborate which left Isla wondering what he'd done to impress Georgio. She caught the direction of her thoughts and felt uncomfortable at her readiness to judge Theo badly. He'd rejected her cruelly but that didn't mean he couldn't behave well to others. Georgio's warmth convinced her it hadn't been just a welcome for a good customer. Had she been too harsh with Theo, always expecting the worst?

'What did he mean by lies about you?'

Theo lifted one dark eyebrow. 'You haven't been following the media?'

'I've had other things on my mind.'

His huff of amusement made her lips curve.

'I can imagine.' He paused. 'There's a lot of finger-pointing about my character and supposed guilt for the death of Costa Stavroulis.'

'But you were cleared. The authorities proved you didn't do it.'

His smile now held little amusement. 'Does something have to be true to make news? Most of them are careful not to accuse me outright but there are plenty of insinuations, gossip, supposed statements from *sources close to the Karalis family…*'

Isla goggled. Once he'd been released from prison she'd stopped following the news.

'But why?'

'The victim was the grandson of Spiro Stavroulis, a media magnate. The old man wants justice for his grandson but until another suspect is identified, he's directing his vitriol at me.'

'That makes no sense if he knows you're innocent.'

'Maybe he didn't believe my alibi was real. Or thinks that in applying pressure, I'll produce the real culprit.'

She shook her head. 'How could you? You're not the police.'

Something shifted in Theo's expression. 'He died in my family home. The night of a farewell party for my mother as she was moving somewhere that suits her needs better. Old Stavroulis probably thinks I've got inside information I'm not sharing.' His jaw tightened. 'He knows I despised his grandson. Costa was a bad influence and I'd warned him away from my stepsister, Toula. I didn't want him hanging around her.'

Theo's tone was harsh and uncompromising. The voice of a man relentless in protecting those he cared for.

Instead of scaring her, Isla was drawn to that. This man would protect his child with the last breath in his body.

She found that impossibly attractive. She wanted that.

For her baby, of course.

Georgio arrived then with a pile of plates balanced on his arms. The food looked and smelled delicious and her appetite, which had been gradually improving, was suddenly back full force.

The next little while was taken up with eating. She

and Theo talked, but only about the food and the location, and with each passing minute she relaxed more.

Maybe it was the warmth of the place and the good food. Maybe because Theo's conversation was easy, as if he wasn't waiting on her decision about his proposal.

Perhaps it was partly because he'd swapped his suit for jeans and a dark green pullover. Even casually dressed Theo had a masculine charisma that couldn't be ignored. Everything about him was attractive. From the hard, compelling lines of his face to that well-defined, sensual mouth and eyes that, when he smiled, reminded her of warm honey. Even the scar near his eye didn't detract from his magnetism.

Worryingly, he looked more like the man she'd fallen in love with than someone who'd destroyed her trust.

Isla sought something to say that would take her mind off him without leading back to the baby and marriage. She didn't want to argue about that tonight.

'Is that pullover hand-knitted? It's a distinctive design.' It had clearly been made to fit his athletic frame. If Theo ever ditched his suits in favour of pullovers, knitwear sales would soar.

Theo's expression softened as he glanced down. 'It is handmade. You've got a good eye.'

'I *do* work in a knitting shop.'

'Does that mean you knit? I don't remember seeing you working with wool.'

When they'd met, she'd had other things to occupy her. Isla's blood quickened at the memories and she hoped that wasn't a blush she felt.

'I've knitted since I was a child.'

One of the carers in the home had taught her one Christmas. It had been a diversion from the fact that their festive season wasn't terribly festive. Isla had been fascinated with the idea of making something from simply a string of wool, plus she'd found it comforting, the steady rhythm of the needles taking the edge off her loneliness. Even surrounded by other orphans there were times when she'd felt utterly separate.

'What are you thinking, Isla? You've gone somewhere else in your head.'

She was about to deny it then stopped herself. Withdrawing from others, even turning away before they had a chance to reject her, had become habit. The exception had been with Theo. Her mouth twisted. Look what had happened then. Yet there was no need to be so defensive. They had to build bridges to sort out their child's future.

She had to trust him more and put aside her wariness.

'I was thinking about how I took to knitting as a kid. I made woollen scarves for everyone I knew.' Someone had donated a lot of wool so she had plenty to work with. 'By the time I was in my teens I was making hats, scarves and other things to sell at a neighbourhood market. Earning my own money was a great incentive.'

'You don't knit for yourself?'

'Sometimes. But there's a good market for quality handmade pieces. I take orders from people who want something unique for themselves or as a special gift. It's not a get-rich-quick scheme because of the work involved. But I find it soothing and any money is welcome when you're a student.'

Not that she was a student now. The reminder dragged the smile off her face.

Theo didn't seem to notice. 'You have a lot in common with my mother.'

'Sorry? How?'

'For a start, she knitted this for me.'

He sat straighter as if to show off the fine work. His patent pride dissolved the restriction she'd placed around her heart. It was sweet that he felt that way about his mother.

Excitement stirred. That's what she hoped for with her child. She hugged the precious idea close.

'Your mother's very talented. I wouldn't mind the pattern.'

'You can ask for it when you see her. She'll be back in Athens soon.' Before Isla could wonder about the possibility of meeting Theo's mother, he went on. 'When I was a kid she knitted my pullovers and sewed my clothes. Every night I'd go to sleep to the sound of her knitting needles clacking. Like you, she made extra money making clothes for other people.'

Isla sat back, stunned, not by the fact his mother had made money that way but by the sudden connection she felt to a woman she'd never met. She too had known hardship, far more than Isla. At least Isla had always had a roof over her head.

Both of them had a soft spot for this man. In his mother's case it was inevitable. In Isla's it was a weakness, yet tonight she couldn't find the determination to thrust him away. The knowledge settled in her with something that felt strangely like relief.

'She'll enjoy meeting you, I know.'

'She knows about me?'

Theo shook his head. 'Not yet. I thought you needed time to rest and acclimatise.' He paused, holding her gaze and when he spoke it was in a deep voice that sounded sincere. 'I didn't want to push you into meeting her too soon. I know I've asked a lot of you, Isla. I know this isn't easy.'

He moved closer and the warmth of his gaze melted another layer of her defences. Soon she'd have none left against him.

She'd done nothing but think about him, yearn for him, even dream about him, since he'd walked back into her life. She'd clung to anger as a defence mechanism but lately, seeing Theo not as an enemy but as someone considerate and patient, it had stopped working. Keeping her distance was increasingly difficult.

'I'm glad you're here, Isla.'

The sincerity in his voice and the look in his gilded eyes reminded her of the intimacies they'd shared. Intimacies she missed so much.

'I'm only here because I'm pregnant. You wouldn't have come after me if not for that.'

Theo didn't respond immediately and she saw something in his expression she didn't understand. A hint of strong emotion. Then he seemed to stiffen, his features setting in hard planes as he lifted his shoulders. 'I was needed here. That had to be my priority.' He paused. 'Would you rather I lied about that?'

'No!' Isla surveyed him, astonished to discover his frankness brought a sense of freedom, though once her bruised ego would have protested his words. She'd rather have brutal truth than deceive herself with lies. 'I only want honesty. I don't want anything else from you.'

'Nothing at all?'

She was about to reiterate that she wasn't interested in wealth or power when his hand covered hers on the table.

Instantly familiar sensations bombarded her. Not

merely the warmth and sense of rightness in his touch. But that trembling, eager feeling deep inside.

Of course she wanted more.

Theo Karalis had feet of clay. He wasn't the ideal man she dreamed about. But she wanted him with an abiding need nothing could obliterate. Not disillusionment nor pride nor willpower.

Isla huffed a silent laugh that felt like a groan.

What willpower? She inhaled his scent, drawing in his heat and strength, senses sparking in the newly charged atmosphere between them, and couldn't pull back.

She'd struggled not to be drawn in by his spell. It was a losing battle.

'Isla? Speak to me.'

For the first time she detected real uncertainty in him. Did he too fight not to succumb to the pull between them? She'd told herself Theo was immune and didn't feel that desire any more. But reading his taut features and the slight unsteadiness in his hand, it hit her that she wasn't alone in this.

'To say what?'

His gaze scorched her. 'That you want me. As much as I want you.'

Isla moistened dry lips, knowing how much rode on her answer. She must have hesitated too long for abruptly Theo withdrew, scraping his chair back from the table as if needing to put as much distance between them as possible.

'Sorry. I don't want to pressure you. I keep forgetting you're sick when you look so…' Theo shook his head. 'I'm out of line—'

'You're not out of line.' Caution died with his withdrawal. 'You're right.'

Her breath caught as, instead of triumph in those gleaming eyes, she read relief, crowded out a moment later by excitement. His expression was raw and hungry and it matched exactly what she felt.

'For the record I'm not sick. I feel better than I have in ages.' The enforced rest had restored a lot of her strength.

Something crackled in the air. That lightning spark of sexual connection that had arced between them from the first. The fine hairs on Isla's arms stood on end, her breasts felt fuller and pressed against her bra where her nipples peaked.

Did Theo notice? His nostrils flared as if he scented her arousal. Far from feeling shy about it, Isla experienced an upswell of pride and confidence.

Why shouldn't she admit to desire? Why shouldn't she satisfy it? They both understood the situation. This wasn't about romance. Theo had admitted that she wasn't his first priority. But he *had* admitted to wanting her and suddenly that was all she could think about. Easing the gnawing hunger she carried wherever she went.

Surely she was entitled to that at least?

What had she to lose? She'd learned from disillusionment. She wouldn't expect too much this time, just the physical pleasure Theo could give her.

'You want me.'

It wasn't a question. Theo's tone conveyed satisfaction and something she couldn't identify. But Isla wasn't in the business any more of trying to understand Theo's emotions. This was sex, pure and simple.

As for the baby and Theo's outrageous proposition, those decisions were best left to another day. When she could think straight.

'Yes.'

The smile that unfurled across his face made her light-headed. But not as much as when he scooted his chair forward, reaching out and threading his fingers through hers. The electricity in the air was inside her now and she could barely sit still, so potent was his effect.

'I want you, Isla, you have no idea how much.'

He rose, pulling her to her feet. As they crossed the room Giorgio appeared, all smiles, carrying their jackets. Theo helped her into hers, his hands lingering a moment longer than necessary, before he shrugged into his and passed a credit card to their host. Isla was barely aware of what was said, only that Giorgio invited them back. Then they stepped out into the crisp night, Theo taking her hand as they turned down the lane.

Neither spoke. Every sense was focused on what lay ahead. She stumbled and he wrapped his arm around her, pulling her close and steadying her. She felt the urgency rise in him too yet he kept his pace steady, not rushing her over the uneven surface.

Cool air brushed Isla's cheeks but inside an unquenchable fire had ignited, burning low in her body.

So wrapped up was she in the man beside her that she barely noticed a flash of light across the quiet street as he helped her into the car. She had an impression of movement but turned away to look at Theo's proud profile, her heart rising to her throat in anticipation.

The trip to his apartment was a blur. Isla couldn't say whether it took two minutes or twenty. All that mattered was that finally they were alone, the door closed against the outside world.

Her breasts rose and fell with her choppy breathing as Theo locked the door. In Isla's feverish imagination it felt as if that cut them off from the worries of the world.

For this night she was free simply to feel and respond. Tomorrow would be time enough to think about the future and their negotiations.

Theo turned towards her. His face looked different, features pared back, emphasising his magnificent bone structure and that intrinsic, masculine power which she'd always found secretly irresistible. But more important than his charismatic looks was the visceral sensation that being with him was as necessary as breathing.

He reached out his hand and Isla placed hers in it, feeling the inevitable shiver of excitement as his fingers closed around hers.

She'd take tonight and not look back.

CHAPTER NINE

THEO LOOKED AT the woman before him and told himself to go slow. She was still recuperating. Until a few weeks ago she'd been ill every day. She was pregnant, carrying his child in that slim body.

The idea sent a judder of excitement through him, mixed with incredible tenderness and nerves at the idea of doing the wrong thing. Of perhaps hurting her or their baby.

Yet he'd never wanted a woman more than he wanted Isla Jacobs.

She stood there, proud as a goddess, head up, shoulders back, breasts thrust forward against the rich russet of her dress. Theo's hands prickled with the need to reach out and touch her. To skim his palms over those delicate curves. To shape her breasts. To tug her hair free so it spilled around her shoulders like liquid silk. He remembered the scent of it, like rosemary, honey and sunshine. Like endless summer days when everything was right in the world.

He wanted her so much he had to take a moment to gather himself, not simply grab.

Unbidden, memory rose of the moment when they'd reached his car tonight and a paparazzo had appeared.

Theo had got them away quickly and maybe Isla hadn't noticed. But it was a reminder that he'd brought her into his world now and he had to do everything to protect her.

Guilt froze the air in his lungs. Foolish of him to take her out without a security detail, but he'd worked on the basis that, just once, they could slip under the radar without staff around.

There'd be no turning back the tide of curiosity now about her, about *them*. Isla didn't know it yet but it was another reason for her to accept his proposal. As her husband Theo could protect her better against the inevitable tsunami of press intrusion.

Tonight had proved how important that was. When the photographer had appeared, snapping photos of her, Theo had had to fight down the impulse to march over and rip the camera away. It was something he'd never done despite plenty of provocation.

He could handle anything that was thrown at him, but a possible threat to Isla was a whole new ballgame.

Theo breathed deep, forcing air into cramped lungs.

No time now for worrying about the press. Already his thoughts scattered as he took in the heavy rise and fall of her breasts and the flush of excitement in her sweet face.

He walked towards her, stiff from the way every muscle in his body pulled tight. Plus there was the erection he'd battled all through the journey home.

Her stunning eyes, the colour of early-morning mist over the sea, held his and he recognised the gift she offered. Gone were the recriminations and doubts. She met his stare appraisingly, as an equal.

Need scythed through him, a white-hot blade, taking him right up to her two long strides. 'I'm sorry.'

'About what?'

He was already bending, one arm around her back and the other behind her knees, sweeping her up into his embrace. 'This. You bring out the caveman in me.'

Theo had intended to take her hand and lead her to the bedroom like an urbane, civilised lover but some primitive part of his brain urged him to take control in this most fundamental way. Gather her to him, as if he feared she might disappear like a mirage. As she had all those nights when she'd featured in his dreams, only to vanish, leaving him bereft.

His heart knocked his ribs as he held her close, her face upturned to his.

'Don't apologise. I like it.' Her voice, husky with need, stroked through him, sending his senses into overdrive. She reached up to thread her fingers through his hair then clasp the back of his neck as if she needed to stake her claim.

Adrenaline shot through his bloodstream at the idea and he found himself grinning.

Her soft body nestled against him as he strode to his bedroom. With each step his heartbeat revved faster.

Soon. Soon. Soon.

There was no need to pause and switch on a light. The curtains hadn't been drawn and silvery moonlight spilled across the bed from the huge windows that gave a spectacular view of the city.

Theo stopped beside the king-sized bed and made himself put her down. Of course it wasn't that simple. He was reluctant to release her so he did it slowly, turning the inch-by-inch slide of her body into slow-motion torture and bliss.

A gasp sounded loud in the silence. His or hers, he

didn't know. He felt them both stop breathing at that exquisite friction.

Finally she stood between his feet, the bed behind her, but Theo kept his hands on her hips. Not because she was unsteady but because he couldn't seem to release her.

Mine, mine, mine, the greedy voice inside his head chanted. His blood throbbed to the beat of it. His snatched breaths matched it too.

Until his brain began to work. Zips, buttons, shoes. Barriers to what they both wanted. Barriers he wanted to strip instantly, but he made himself pretend he was civilised. A man who understood that tearing his lover's clothes from her body might be scary, even for a woman trembling with a need that matched his.

That tiny sign of Isla's desperation, despite her proud stance, tugged at emotions far deeper than lust. Emotions he'd take time to analyse later. When he could think straight.

'Take your hair down, Isla.'

She didn't hesitate and that was another punch of arousal to his already heightened senses.

Theo watched the glorious waves tumble around her shoulders, her beckoning scent stronger now. Or perhaps he was even more attuned.

'Perfect.' His voice was a rumbling growl that should have scared her. Instead, her lips parted as if she too were so aroused she found it difficult to catch her breath.

Theo's fingers flexed. 'Now the dress.'

Was that a pout? His pulse was a driving beat deep in his groin as she slipped her tongue across her bottom lip and he fought to smother a groan.

'You don't want to take it off me?'

Theo imagined doing it. Not questing for the zip at her

side, but fastening his big hands on the delicately draped neckline and tugging to rip it apart from neck to hem, revealing Isla in all her glory.

His throat was lined with sandpaper as he tried to swallow. 'It's better if you do it. Faster.'

Fathomless eyes surveyed him from that uptilted face. 'Only if you take your pullover off.'

Theo lifted his arms and wrenched it up over his head. By the time Isla had found her zip and undone it he was naked from the waist up, the night air a relief against burning skin. Was she deliberately going slow to tease him? More likely his movements were rushed.

He stepped back, giving her space as he removed his shoes and socks. Straightening, he was in time to see her shimmy out of the dark red dress. It dropped to the floor like his plunging stomach as he drank in the sight of her.

'So perfect,' he whispered hoarsely. Despite her recent weight loss she was stunning.

When he looked at her face again Isla held his gaze and even in the moonlight he felt the gut-deep slam of connection. Like the unseen but palpable waves of energy radiating from an explosion. He almost expected to hear the reverberating boom of detonation.

When her hand moved to cover her belly he was surprised. Could she possibly think her pregnancy marred her sensual perfection? Or was it a gesture born of protectiveness?

Either way it pierced his swelling satisfaction.

'You don't believe me?'

'None of us are perfect.'

Finally her hand fell away. There it was, the beginnings of a baby bump. A rush of emotion surged through him. More than desire, more than appreciation.

Theo dropped to his knees, his fingers reaching for the waistband of her tights. He paused, his breath hissing at the delicious shock of her smooth, bare skin against his knuckles as he slipped his fingers inside the stretchy fabric and drew it down her hips.

The scent of her was different here. Earthier, more decidedly feminine, beckoning him with the evidence of her arousal.

He moved quickly, rolling the fabric past the narrow band of her black lace knickers, down her silky thighs, past her knees to her shins, her slender ankles. His heart knocked hard when she planted her fingertips on his shoulders for balance as she lifted first one foot then the other so he could strip the tights away.

Theo skimmed his palms back up to that inviting band of lace. But his patience wore thin and a second later he'd yanked the delicate material down so hard it pooled around her ankles. She shifted her weight, one thigh moving forward a little as if instinctively protecting her modesty.

He shook his head, circling his hand around her thigh and gently tugging it wide. Silently he drank in the treasure revealed. The pale swathe of her abdomen, where a precious new life nestled. The dark V of soft hair guarding her femininity.

The female body, *Isla's body*, was the most wonderful, remarkable thing in the world. And the most arousing. Theo's jaw set hard and aching as he tried to hold on to control.

He looked up, meeting her eyes. 'Now the bra. Take it off.'

Her lips moved, her expression just the right side of mutinous. 'What about the rest of *your* clothes?'

'Soon. First I need you naked.'

His voice was harsh but Isla didn't seem to mind.

Theo had believed he already enjoyed the finest view possible, until she reached back and undid the black lace bra, letting it slide down her arms and freeing her breasts to sway above him.

Was it possible to come just from looking at a woman?

He felt so close, so aroused that for long seconds he couldn't move. Finally, with a shuddering breath he closed the distance between them. Hands gently cradling her bare hips, he kissed her belly. A tiny, fervent yet featherlight kiss right above their baby. Then more kisses, gentle and full of wonderment and desire.

He tightened his grip as she sighed and he felt her wobble as if her knees loosened. He knew the feeling, he was experiencing it right now.

'Easy, *glykia mou*.' His breath feathered her skin and she quivered anew, her hands anchoring on his bare shoulders. Even that simple touch felt like a gift.

As for Isla, she was a miracle. He couldn't imagine wanting another woman the way he did her. Because of the baby she carried? No, it was more than that. Impending motherhood merely added to her potent allure.

Theo skimmed his lips across her abdomen, intrigued by the swell of her pregnancy. Then he kissed his way down to the silky thatch of chestnut hair, nuzzling as he went.

He heard her call his name but because of the rush of blood in his ears he couldn't tell if it was a question or a plea. He slid one hand between her thighs, a grunt of satisfaction escaping as she widened her stance, allowing him access. She was slippery, ready for him, and his erection rose against the confines of his trousers. He was so needy it physically hurt but this wasn't the time for urgent sex.

Theo reminded himself she was pregnant, of the need to be especially gentle. He ignored the ache in his groin, the sense that his lower body had turned leaden, and concentrated on her.

His questing touch reached her clitoris and she stiffened, fingers tightening on his shoulders. As he delved further and deeper, she shuddered and sighed, her pelvis tilting up the way a sunflower follows bright light.

Isla was that light for him, always drawing him. He knew that if he hadn't been locked up in prison, he'd never have been able to keep his distance, even knowing their separation was for the best.

But now there was nothing keeping them apart. His scruples and fears about involving her in his life meant nothing now she carried their child. She belonged with him and he intended to prove it to her.

He smiled as he leaned in and kissed her intimately, drawing in her scent and taste. Slowly he feasted, taking his time, not like the starving man he was, who'd gone without for so long. Instead, he savoured every exquisite sensation and above all Isla's responses.

He knew she had doubts about marriage and them being a family, but he'd win her over. One way or another.

Mouth still on her, he looked up and saw her, head thrown back, breasts thrust forward, looking wild and beautiful. He'd never known a more enthralling woman. Sweet and tender yet determined and with a core of strength that made her all the more alluring.

With or without the baby she was a woman worth winning.

She looked down, their gazes meshing, heat saturated

him at their powerful, erotic connection. He drew on her soft flesh and she shuddered. He felt the tiny tremble begin low in her body and did it again.

Her fingers threaded his hair, clamping his skull as she tilted into his caress. His senses were full of her arousal, exacerbating his own need.

'Theo!' It was a cry of exultation and surrender as her body grew taut as a drawn bow, still for just a moment, before completion crashed upon her and he gathered her close as she shivered in ecstasy.

When the shudders stopped he nudged her towards the bed. The backs of her legs touched the mattress and she collapsed onto it. The dreamy bliss on Isla's face told him everything he needed to know. As did her pale arm reaching out for him.

Isla's body had turned to jelly and her soul to radiant light. Theo had given her ecstasy but far more too.

Crazy as it sounded to what was left of her logical mind, it felt as if he'd given back something precious that had been destroyed with his deceit and rejection.

His tenderness made her throat catch. The reverence of his kneeling form before her, his expression of wonder as he'd surveyed her…

She'd known he was thinking of their baby, of the marvel of new life they'd created. Then, when he kissed her there, she'd felt utterly precious. It was a sensation beyond anything she'd experienced and it vanquished her doubts, as surely as if he'd melted an armoury of bristling weapons, turning them into molten gold.

Some men would have been horrified by an unexpected pregnancy. Theo's uninhibited delight in both her news and her body undid every defence. If she hadn't already been impatient for his lovemaking, that would have won her over.

Isla's body floated on the wide bed. But she found the energy to reach out an arm in invitation because, wonderful as that had been, she needed more. She needed Theo.

He stood beside the bed, hands clenched as if resisting the impulse to touch her.

'I should get a condom.'

'It's a bit late for that.' Then she bit her lip. She'd momentarily forgotten that protection wasn't just against pregnancy. 'Unless you…?'

'There's been no one since you, Isla.'

It shouldn't surprise her, after all he'd been locked away for months. Yet he'd been free for some time. A man with Theo's looks, charisma and wealth would have no trouble attracting women and surely he'd been tempted to celebrate his freedom from incarceration.

Yet she believed him. Everything she learned about him told her he was a man who'd protect those he cared for. He might only care for her as the mother of his unborn child but he would keep her safe.

'Then come here. I need you to hold me.'

She'd missed Theo's arms around her, his heart beating against hers and his powerful body sheltering her. Besides, despite the glittering climax he'd bestowed, her body still throbbed eagerly. He'd taken the edge off her need but she wanted him, wanted them together.

The bed dipped as he lay beside her, turning her towards him and surveying her intently. His back was to the window so his face was in shadow, yet Isla *felt* his scrutiny as sure as touch.

She palmed his cheek, feeling his flesh twitch in response. He radiated heat and pent-up tension. When she slid her hand down his neck and across his shoulder she found every inch rigid. His breathing was harsh and uneven.

Everything told her he fought to rein himself in, his need so powerful she wondered if perhaps he didn't trust himself. Otherwise why hold back? There'd never been reticence in their lovemaking and Isla had learned the joys of sexual power and sensual abandon with him as well as the most beguiling tenderness.

'Theo? What is it?'

He breathed deep, the hair on his chest tickling her nipples and sending a shaft of desire straight to her womb.

'I don't want to hurt you or the baby.'

Her breath snared. His concern and hesitation moved her. He didn't act like the uncaring man she'd once painted him, someone who used and discarded people at his convenience.

Isla's heart swelled. 'You're not going to hurt us. I want you.'

I need you.

But she bit her lip so as not to let those words escape.

She shuffled towards him, closing the space between them and a gasp ripped through the night air. His large hand settled on her waist, his knee nudging between her thighs. 'I don't think I can hold back.'

'Good.' Then her breath fractured as his hand moved to her sensitive breast and her eyes rolled back at the perfection of his touch. No other man had ever affected her so.

Yet instead of pushing her onto her back and moving over her, Theo slid his hand around her knee and lifted her leg over his hip, tugging her close until she felt his hard shaft between her legs. They lay on their sides facing each other and she was completely open to him. Even then he didn't move immediately but those seconds of waiting only fuelled her hunger.

He guided himself so she felt the blunt head of his erection against her and couldn't prevent herself moving, seeking all that masculine strength she longed for.

'Isla.' He whispered her name as she planted her palm on his broad chest to feel his heart thrumming as fast as hers.

With one slow, sure thrust Theo brought them together. It had been so long and it felt so utterly perfect that for a second Isla forgot how to breathe. Instantly he stopped, as if trying to gauge if her response was from discomfort. But when she angled her pelvis towards him, hooking her heel harder behind him to bring them together, all hesitancy vanished.

In an instant he was the strong, accomplished lover she remembered. He took command of their rhythm and her body. His guttural words of praise stoked her arousal, as did his ability to find exactly the right spot, deep inside, where she most needed him.

Then, just as she thought this couldn't get any better, he leaned in and kissed her.

Isla had forgotten how flagrantly erotic a kiss could be. How perfect the sense of communion between two mouths, two bodies moving as one.

Pleasure was a gift equally shared as she gave him back caress for caress, holding him close as if their joined bodies might fly apart unless she held on tight.

His mouth was dark velvet. His body a force of nature, consuming yet revitalising her, making her feel helpless in the face of such power but at the same time stronger and more alive than she'd ever been. As if he stripped her back to bare essentials then revealed something in herself more profound than she'd ever recognised.

Through it all were those threads of pleasure, weaving through her body, unravelling, bunching, but finally coming together in beautiful patterns that presaged bliss and the ultimate mystery between a man and a woman.

Isla felt everything coalesce, every sensation, every emotion and fear was part of it, part of her.

She cried his name as the thundering roar of pleasure bore down on her again. This time, wonderfully, he was there with her, his body urging her on, his mouth swallowing her sob of fulfilment. Wave upon wave of ecstasy broke through her and she clutched him close. Then, just as she found her peak, Theo's powerful body shuddered in her embrace, the hot liquid of his climax pulsing deep.

Incredible tenderness filled her as she gathered him to her. He groaned and called her name, the sound muffled in the sensitive curve between her shoulder and neck.

Finally their breathing eased, their taut bodies slumping together in sated abandon. She didn't have the energy to move even if she wanted to and she knew with a clarity that would have shocked her mere hours before, that there was nowhere in the world she'd rather be than here, like this, with Theo.

It felt as if the world had been shattered and remade by what they'd shared.

As she drifted into sleep Isla told herself it was an illusion. What felt to her like love was merely sex. She couldn't make the mistake of reading too much into it.

All that had changed was her pregnancy. She had

to remember that and not fall into the trap of romantic fantasies.

From now on she'd be sensible and pragmatic with Theo. Starting tomorrow.

CHAPTER TEN

SEVERAL HOURS LATER, Isla leaned back, relaxing in the warm water that came up almost to her collarbone. She spread her arms along the edge of the wide bath and felt every muscle in her body soften.

'You look like the cat that got the cream.'

The deep voice burred across her skin. Despite her floating feeling, as if her well-used body couldn't possibly move again, her nipples tightened.

Maybe she wasn't quite as exhausted as she'd thought.

She opened her eyes and there was Theo at the other end of the massive, sunken bath, his eyes glowing like embers as he surveyed her.

'I'm not the only one.' He looked like a man well-satisfied with his lot.

He sat higher than her, the impressive spread of his shoulders and muscled arms evident above the water. His chest, broad and leanly muscled as if from athletic exercise rather than steroids or pumping weights, glistened. The dark hair across his pectorals was wet and Isla remembered how that felt against her skin from the night they'd made love months ago during a moonlit swim.

A coil of heat circled low in her body. Definitely not as tired as she'd imagined. Or maybe she simply responded to this feeling of utter, physical well-being. She'd woken to darkness in Theo's vast bed, alone. Realising he'd left her, the gloss of satisfaction had worn off. Till he appeared in the doorway, naked and compelling, to ask if she felt like a restorative bath.

She'd barely said yes when he hoisted her into his arms and carried her into the most stunning bathroom she'd ever seen. Even here there was a panoramic view of the city. Yet it wasn't that or the luxurious fittings that caught her attention. It was the array of candles set around the room, bathing it in a soft glow, and the vast sunken tub, an invitation to decadence. All evidence that Theo had exerted himself to make this nice for her.

You're going to be sensible and pragmatic, her head reminded her.

Her heart squeezed. She wanted to be anything but sensible. But she owed it to her baby not to be swept away by a romantic gesture.

Her gaze narrowed on Theo's chiselled features, trying to read his thoughts. 'The scar. How did you get that?'

In the heat it looked more livid than usual and she swallowed, registering how close it was to his eye.

He shrugged, sending a ripple of warm water to lap around her bare body. 'A recent altercation.'

Isla frowned. Theo had never revealed a temper or the sort of antagonistic masculinity that sometimes led to fights. She couldn't imagine him provoking violence. Then enlightenment dawned. 'Someone hurt you while you were locked up?'

After a moment he nodded. 'It wasn't a safe place.'

There was something in his tone, irony and understatement, a bitterness she'd never heard from him before. Who wouldn't be bitter, locked up for a crime they hadn't committed?

'I thought the authorities would protect people in a remand centre. After all you hadn't been convicted.'

Another flash of stark emotion in those stormy eyes. 'I wasn't in a remand centre, I was in a high-security prison. And no matter how good the security, there's always a way around it.'

Isla's heart beat high against her throat. 'How did it happen?' She couldn't imagine him deliberately threatening another prisoner.

Theo shook his head. 'It doesn't matter. It's in the past.'

She slid her arms down and wrapped them around her torso. The image of some hardened criminal attacking him, and by the look of that scar with some sort of weapon, made her feel sick. She knew it would haunt her.

That was why she found herself crossing a boundary she'd vowed not to go near. 'You say you want marriage, yet you won't share that small thing with me. How do you expect me to contemplate marriage if you shut me out? That's not how marriages work, even the sort you're suggesting.'

Not that she was seriously considering marriage, that would be a recipe for disaster, with her craving more than he could give. But Isla wasn't above using his outrageous proposition to satisfy her curiosity. Though it didn't feel like idle curiosity. Her fear when she thought of him being attacked ran too deep.

A vertical line appeared in the centre of his forehead. 'You're right.' He paused. 'I'm used to keeping trouble to myself. But since it's important to you…'

His eyes held hers and Isla felt that powerful tug of connection. Too late she wondered at the wisdom of calling him on this. Weren't there things she didn't want to share, most notably her feelings for him? She was about to tell him it didn't matter when he spoke.

'I had a price on my head in prison and someone decided to claim that reward.'

'What do you mean a price?' Surely he hadn't been there long enough to make enemies.

'It was common knowledge that Spiro Stavroulis would pay handsomely to anyone who injured me badly enough. He's the grandfather of the man I was supposed to have killed.'

Her stomach hollowed. She wanted to object that Theo was innocent, then remembered what he'd said about Stavroulis wanting a scapegoat. What must it have been like for Theo, locked away for something he didn't do, surrounded by violent men, under threat?

Isla drew her knees up and wrapped her arms tight around them, hunching into herself at the thought.

She heard whispered swearing and then there was a wave of water as Theo moved to her end of the bath. He sat beside her, bare hip to bare hip, one arm around her, pulling her against his solid torso. She went willingly, glad for the contact. It was a comfort having him here, so obviously alive and well.

'I *knew* I shouldn't have told you.'

'Of course you should. I'd rather know the truth than be left in the dark.' She lifted her head and met his gaze. 'Was it a knife?'

After a moment he nodded. 'An improvised one with a razor blade.'

Isla blinked, trying to clear the image her mind conjured. 'I'm so sorry.'

'There's nothing to be sorry about. You're right, I need to let you in more if we're to have a future together.'

It was on the tip of Isla's tongue to tell him they didn't have a future, not in the way he wanted, but she didn't say it. For suddenly she found she wasn't as vehemently opposed to marriage as she should be.

Taking comfort in his closeness, reliving the horror of his danger and now feeling a rush of relief, she faced the strength of her feelings for Theo. Despite what she'd told herself in London, those hadn't changed.

Could she really be thinking of marrying him?

Surely not. She cared too much for him while he…

She shivered. This time she couldn't tell if the tremor was from trepidation or something else. What she *did* know was that, despite the past, he was important to her.

She lifted her hand to trace the scar. 'I'm glad you're safe.'

Theo captured her hand and pressed a kiss to her palm, his eyes holding hers. 'So am I. I'd much rather be here with you.'

His crooked smile said volumes about that experience but she'd pressed him enough.

'Thank you for telling me.' It might be a straightforward story but Isla felt his sharing it with her was significant. Like when he'd told her about his childhood, but this time it was something he'd got no benefit from sharing. The information about his family had been part of his plan to persuade her into marriage.

'You're right. We need to understand each other better. In the past we shared a lot but on reflection we never discussed anything truly important.' He grinned. 'Except for the love of your life—archaeology.'

A smile tickled Isla's mouth. 'And the love of yours—football.'

He was right. They'd talked a lot, getting to know each other, but for all those conversations they'd never delved deep. The true sense of connection had come in other ways, when they made love, but also in the mutual understanding that hadn't seemed to need words.

'While we're sharing… There's something I want to ask you.'

Slowly Isla nodded, mentally readying herself for a question about her opposition to marrying him.

'You said you didn't know your parents and that you were brought up by someone else. Were you adopted or fostered out? Who raised you?'

Isla felt her jaw slacken. Theo had seemed so single-minded, going to so much trouble to persuade her into marriage. Why deviate from that? Knowing about her childhood wouldn't get him closer to that goal and he was a man who focused on achieving his goals.

Her childhood was a cold, disappointing place that she tried not to revisit often. It would be easy to shrug off his question but she didn't. Because what she'd said about Theo not sharing applied to her as well.

Isla had never opened up to Theo about truly personal stuff like her childhood and had steered conversations away from that. It was a habit she'd acquired early, never voluntarily discussing her upbringing. She wasn't ashamed of her past yet was cautious in talking about it. As if by admitting out loud that she'd never been loved, she might invite others to view her as unlovable too.

It was a secret fear she'd hoarded to herself. Perhaps her greatest fear.

Theo felt the tension in her slender body and pulled her closer. He supposed it would be easier to avoid difficult topics and from her reaction earlier he knew this was a difficult topic. But ever since she'd made that dismissive remark about her childhood he'd burned to know more. Not because information was power and the more he knew about Isla the more able he'd be to convince her to marry. His curiosity wasn't strategic. He simply wanted to understand and, he realised, be there for her. Instinct told him that in Isla's case her childhood loss was still very real.

So he didn't retract the question, despite seeing the shutters come down in her eyes and feeling her flinch. Instead he waited.

'Mainly I was brought up in an orphanage.'

'An orphanage?' He'd imagined her as a pretty child, adopted easily. 'I thought you'd have been in a private home.'

'Adoption?' She shook her head. 'It's not always so easy, especially for older children.'

He frowned. Had he misunderstood? 'I thought you lost your parents when you were a baby.'

Instantly he knew he'd said the wrong thing as she stiffened.

'I didn't lose them so much as they lost me.' Her mouth twisted and she turned away, looking towards the window. 'I was abandoned as a newborn. No note, no memento, no name, just me wrapped in a blanket in a box.'

An ache tightened Theo's throat at the idea of a tiny infant left to the mercy of strangers. He pulled Isla fully into his arms to sit sideways on his lap, his arm around her back, another around her knees.

'It's okay, Theo. It was a long time ago. I don't remember it.'

That didn't make it any better. His heart thudded against his ribs as he rocked her to him. He tried to imagine their child left in that way but his mind refused to cooperate.

'What happened? They didn't have enough people interested in adoption?' Easier to ask about that than think of that tiny, deserted baby.

'It wasn't that simple. I'm sure they would have tried adoption but it turned out I was born with a heart defect, which meant surgery. That's daunting for anyone, especially people looking for a perfect little baby to make their own.'

Her voice sounded brittle and who could blame her? Theo's anger built but he kept it in.

He thought of the faded scarring he'd seen on her chest and hadn't asked about. At the time he'd been too busy seducing Isla and later, possibly because it was obviously so old, there'd seemed more important things to concentrate on. He wished he'd asked. Would it have unlocked the story of her past? Or was she telling him now because they'd made a baby together and had to negotiate its future?

'So you stayed in an orphanage? What was it like?'

'Not like a home.' Isla leaned her head against him and nestled closer, and warmth spread through him. 'The other kids and I used to watch TV shows about families and it was nothing like where we grew up. But the people there tried. Some of them were really lovely and others were…okay.'

Theo's muscles tightened as he wondered what okay meant. Better for now to take it at face value.

'Actually, that's where I learned to knit.'

He heard the smile in her voice and responded in kind. 'And where you developed your interest in ancient history?' He could imagine her as an eager child, reading stories of Greek myths and hidden treasures.

She raised her hand, stroking her fingers down his chest and sending a ripple of heat through him. Theo fought not to respond, knowing she wasn't intentionally trying to arouse him, though having her seated on his lap didn't help.

'No. I was fostered with a family for a very short time.'

Her hand stopped, fingers splaying against his chest. Theo covered her hand with his.

'It didn't work out?' He made himself focus on her words.

'Oh, it did. I was happy there. They'd already adopted a boy and we felt like a real family. It was the happiest time of my life.'

Her wistful tone made something still within him, for clearly it hadn't *worked.*

Isla leaned back and looked at him. To his surprise her eyes sparkled. 'Martha was a classics lecturer. She told me wonderful stories about ancient Greece and Rome and gave me a book about the old myths that I loved.'

Now he understood that smile. 'She's the one who lit that spark in you, isn't she? The one who got you interested in ancient history and archaeology.'

'Absolutely. She made it come alive but at the same

time spoke about all the mysteries still to be uncovered and treasures to be found. How could I fail to be hooked?'

'She must be very proud of you doing so well with your studies.'

To Theo's dismay Isla's smile faded. 'I'm sure she would be. Unfortunately she died soon after. That's why I wasn't adopted, because Martha was diagnosed with an aggressive cancer. Her husband, Mark, had his hands full with his grief and the son they'd already adopted. The idea of adopting me too…' She shook her head.

'I'm sorry, Isla.' The words weren't sufficient. Even he, who'd never met the family, felt the loss. Isla's smile as she remembered Martha said so much about the woman.

'It was terrible,' she confirmed. 'But I'm so glad I met them. Martha in particular was wonderful…'

And would have made a wonderful mother.

Theo sensed the words she didn't say and his heart twisted in sympathy with the little girl who'd wanted a family of her own. He swallowed, his throat rough as he imagined Isla, abandoned at birth then passed over because of her heart defect, hoping to belong in this family, only to have that hope snatched away.

He remembered how he'd preached to her about the importance of parents, a stable family environment, and cringed.

'It's all right, Theo. It was a long time ago.'

Just because something was in the past didn't mean it couldn't still affect you. Theo couldn't help but think of his stepsister, whose bad choices, especially when it came to men and her recent drug use were, he was sure, linked to her early experiences. Not that there was any evidence of such problems with Isla. On the contrary, she seemed one of the most grounded people he'd met.

'What are you thinking?' She tilted her head to one side, surveying him. 'You have the strangest look on your face.'

'Do I? I was just thinking how remarkable you are.'

The hint of humour in her expression faded. 'Why? We orphans are just like everybody else.'

She'd misinterpreted his sympathy. 'I mean that a lot of people would feel bitter about missing out on a family.' The idea of it made him pause. 'Yet instead of bitterness, you remember that time with fondness and a smile. I think that shows strength of character and I admire it.' He paused. 'I admire *you*.'

He felt terribly sorry for her but knew admitting that wouldn't be welcome. She'd made it clear she didn't want his sympathy and he'd abide by her wishes. And it was true, though she didn't want to know it, that he was impressed with the way she'd put herself through university and gone so far towards achieving her career goals, without the backup and encouragement of family.

'Thank you, Theo. That's…nice.'

Nice? Hardly, not when she was herself remarkable. But he didn't say it, knowing she was wary of what she might see as empty flattery.

Her hand stroked lightly towards his hip and he couldn't help a shiver of response. Guilt bit him. Here she was, sharing her personal history, a history he guessed she rarely talked about, and he was getting a hard-on.

'Is something wrong? You look uncomfortable.'

Theo shifted, trying to conceal the effect she had on him.

'I'm fine. But it's getting late. You need your sleep.'

Though she seemed much better than in England, Isla was still recuperating from months of sickness and exhaustion.

'You're tired?' She drew a deep breath, making Theo too aware off her pink-tipped breasts cresting the water.

Reawakened desire was a bolt of energy, arcing through his body and making his blood pump harder.

Theo was about to make some noncommittal response about needing to work the next day—only too true, given the recent scandal's fallout on his reputation and by extension the company's—when he caught Isla's expression.

Her eyes were knowing, her mouth in an almost-pout that made his grip tighten on her soft flesh.

She was *teasing* him?

It had been so long since they'd shared light-hearted banter and in the interim, life had filled with sombre troubles and responsibilities. Since his arrest, he'd thought of Isla as someone to be protected. His responsibility.

But she was much more, this living, breathing siren.

'I was thinking of you.'

Yet as he spoke, Theo couldn't resist the temptation to trail his hand slowly up her thigh. Satisfaction stabbed as she shivered and leaned into him.

'Do that again.' The words held a throaty edge that rolled through his belly, drawing every nerve tight in anticipation.

Theo splayed his hand across the top of her thigh, his thumb brushing the gossamer-soft hair that hid her feminine core. She shivered again, leaning into his body, her nipples pebbling as if eager for his attention.

Her straying hand moved between them, deft fingers

caressing then encircling his erection, and fire scorched every half-formed thought.

'Isla.' It sounded like a warning and a plea, not surprising as he was torn between sexual need and the voice telling him to hold back.

'Theo. You *do* want me, don't you?'

He laughed, the sound abrupt. 'Can't you tell? I thought it was obvious.'

He pushed her thighs apart, sliding his hand down to cup her. Instantly she tilted her hips, seeking his touch and satisfaction blasted through him. Just like before, she couldn't deny the fierce hunger between them. She seemed to revel in it.

He thought of his plan to persuade her into marriage for the sake of their child. But this wasn't a deliberate tactic to win her over. This was simply…essential.

Plans and persuasion could wait. The forces driving him were too elemental.

'You're not too tired?' Was he crazy, trying to talk her out of this? But much as he craved her sweet surrender, a stronger imperative was at work, the need to protect his woman.

'Tired?' Her grip firmed as she stroked his length, eyes shining as she registered his body's response. 'Do I look tired?'

'You look amazing.'

She stared rapt, as if he were something more than an ordinary man. She made him feel ten feet tall.

Her parted lips were an invitation to delight. The damp heat had turned her hair into a sexy tangle of chestnut curls and where they lay, wet against her pale shoulders, they drew his gaze down to her beautiful breasts. Did he imagine they were fuller than before? Was that due to her pregnancy, or was it his imagination?

Theo's hands went to her waist, gripping firmly and lifting her to face him. Her hands went to his shoulders, those lush breasts bobbing before him.

'Sit astride me.' His voice was a gruff command, raw with anticipation, but it didn't matter as she was already setting her knees on either side of his hips.

She rose and he leaned forward, capturing one berry-tipped breast in his mouth. She tasted of summer sunshine and sweet woman. Her moan of pleasure was the best music he'd ever heard as he drew on her, slow and hard, watching her head tilt back as her pelvis circled and her hands clawed at his shoulders.

'Theo. That feels…'

Her words stopped as he pulled her lower body closer, the apex of her thighs against his erection. That connection blasted away any pretence of him being in control. His hands moved to her hips, insistent, as his hips rose, bringing them even closer.

A great shudder ripped through him. It felt like years since he'd had her. Not an hour. The need for her, a potent brew of sensual expectation and primitive compulsion, eclipsed all else.

'Come to me.' Again it wasn't a lover's smooth invitation but a grunted command, all he could manage as his larynx shut down.

She didn't need further urging, positioning herself above him then sinking low just as he rose again, unable to keep still. One urgent slide was all it took and they were joined, so deep and sure it shocked him.

Had it possibly felt so good last time? His hands found Isla's breasts and she jerked against him, making a sound in the back of her throat that would make a grown man weep with excitement if he weren't fully occupied trying to hold himself still. He'd meant to go slower, cautious of the new life she carried.

But Isla destroyed all thought of holding back and taking it easy. Her hips angled and Theo lodged impossibly deep, at the heart of her. The feel of her slick heat so tight around him, the subtle movement of her muscles drawing at him, shot caution and conscious thought to smithereens.

He squeezed her breast, his other hand clamping her hip as he rose with her. They moved together, finding the primitive rhythm with no effort at all. As if their bodies were totally attuned. Each stroking caress, each breathless coming together was better than the last. His pulse raced harder and faster. The breath sawed from his lungs and the sound of her little gasps of pleasure incited the primitive, desperate man inside him.

They plunged together, riding the surging tide of carnal excitement with growing abandon.

'Come for me, Isla. Let go.'

Because he wanted her to find pleasure, even more than he craved the orgasm he felt bearing down on him like a thundering mountain avalanche.

Once more he bent his head to her breast, closing his mouth around her nipple and sucking till she jerked and cried out, her body clenching hard around him again and again.

Theo wrapped his arms around her, comforting and encouraging her as she came apart, a sense of profound satisfaction blanketing everything else. Until it was too much, the clutching writhe of her body, the way she held his head to her breast, crooning his name over and over as if he'd not only ripped her world apart but put it back together for her.

Whiteout hit. A tsunami of sensation. Heat. Exquisite ecstasy so potent it edged towards pain. Joy so intense it transformed this from sex to something on a new, previously undiscovered plane.

Shudders rocked him and he held Isla close, arms wrapped around her, face buried in the sweet-scented crook of her neck.

He breathed deep, inhaling the tantalising perfume of well-pleasured woman and the tiniest, distinctive trace of rosemary. It was a reminder, not that he needed it, that only with Isla had he ever experienced anything like this.

Because of the baby?

Because of the woman herself?

He'd puzzle it out later. For now all he knew was that Isla belonged with him. He'd do whatever it took to keep her.

CHAPTER ELEVEN

ISLA SLEPT LATE. When she woke, spread-eagled in the centre of Theo's bed, it was to a brilliant blue sky and a sense of wellbeing she hadn't known in forever.

Not since the island, when you were with Theo and wildly in love.

That thought made her breath hitch. She couldn't afford to tumble back into love.

Was it sex that made her feel so good?

From the first Theo had awoken a passionate side of her nature. Yet she felt more than the sated luxury of a blissed-out body.

She thought over last evening, the way they'd connected over their meal out, the barriers they'd broken down as they discussed their lives, each reaching beyond the usual limits to share with the other. That felt significant, as if they really were opening up to each other on a new level as equals.

Was she looking through rose-tinted glasses, seeing what she wanted to see? A cynic would say Theo was motivated by the need to flatten her defences and make her feel they could create a meaningful relationship. Because he wanted marriage, or more specifically, a permanent relationship with his child.

The optimist in her cringed at that view, protesting that last night had been real, both the camaraderie and the joy, and that Theo cared. She'd seen his expression when she'd revealed her past, understanding the sympathy he held in check. His admiration had buoyed her too.

Isla wanted to believe it had all been real but given what had happened before, she needed to be cautious. She couldn't read too much into last night. Theo had only been back in her life a short time. Once before she'd made the error of believing they shared something meaningful and wouldn't make that mistake again.

As for anything more, it was too soon even to consider his suggestion of marriage. Her lips quirked. She couldn't think of it as a proposal, for that implied hearts, flowers and romance. Not something utterly pragmatic.

Besides, she had a sinking feeling she could all too readily fall for Theo again whereas she knew he was focused on practicalities. He was driven by duty and responsibility. Yes, there was caring as well but not the soul-deep adoration she craved.

Was it unrealistic to want that? As long as she could remember she'd yearned for unconditional love. To be the most important person in someone's life, not for pragmatic reasons but just because.

She flung off the sheet and sat up, amazed again that, apart from the tiniest niggle, there was no nausea. She actually felt well. Energised. Fizzing with anticipation.

'Sleep well, *glykia mou*?'

Theo's rich voice curled around her as she entered one of the large sitting rooms. He was sprawled in a large armchair before the huge picture window, phone in hand and computer open nearby. But he wasn't dressed for the office in one of his tailored suits. He wore a dark shirt that somehow emphasised the golden gleam of his eyes, sleeves rolled up casually, and faded jeans.

Isla yanked her gaze back up from those impressive thighs, heat kissing her skin at the memory of Theo's strength. Last night he'd made her feel small and oh-so feminine without in any way diminishing her.

Sexual awareness curled in her belly, the mere sight of him unleashing supercharged, libidinous thoughts.

'Thanks, I did.'

She'd slept a lot since arriving in Athens, though each morning she'd woken knowing her dreams had been uneasy because of her uncertainty about the future. But last night, or rather this morning, her sleep had been deep and restorative.

'You're not going into the office?'

'Not yet. I wanted to be here when you woke.'

Isla had told herself she wasn't disappointed, waking alone in that vast bed. Theo was a busy CEO. No doubt he had teams of people demanding his time. The idea of him letting her sleep in and rescheduling his day to be here for her made her feel special.

'Thank you, Theo.'

Heat flickered in his deep brown eyes, making them glow. Instantly Isla felt an answering heat low in her body. As if it took just one look to bring her to arousal.

But it was true. Isla wanted to snatch his phone away and sink onto Theo's lap, to relive their glorious love-making.

She stiffened, horrified at how much she wanted that and how easily he affected her. How could she withstand this single-minded man if she let herself be tempted so easily?

'I looked in on you a while ago and heard the shower

running so my housekeeper is preparing your breakfast. I'm expecting a conference call then I'll join you.'

Yet he put his phone down and stood, his expression telling her it wasn't business he had on his mind. He was halfway across the room to her when his phone rang and he stopped, cursing under his breath.

For some reason the sight of Theo stymied of his intentions made Isla smile. He might be rich and privileged but in that moment he seemed endearing.

He swung around and stalked back to collect his phone. Isla hurried after him, grabbing his shoulder and planting a swift kiss on his lips before pulling back.

There was a thud as the phone fell. Strong arms wrapped around her, lifting her almost off her feet as Theo kissed her slowly and thoroughly. She sank into him, holding back nothing as their kiss deepened, desire driving them and the world falling away. Finally they separated just enough to breathe properly. Isla's head spun and she heard bells.

'I'd better take it. It's the third time they've rung back.'

Yet Theo didn't release her straightaway. He held her close, eyes intent on hers, and Isla felt something rise within her as if to meet him. Something big and momentous.

Isla shook her head and pushed his shoulders. 'You need to take the call. They're waiting for you.'

She had to remember that one night's sublime intimacy didn't mend the fractures between them. They wanted different things, even if they both wanted the best for their baby.

Finally Theo released her and reached for his phone. 'You're a bad influence, Isla. This is the first time I've ever been tempted to ignore a meeting. You'd better go before I change my mind.'

Despite telling herself it was only a kiss and that nothing was resolved between them, Isla's heart sang as she left the room.

She was sitting in the sunshine on the roof terrace, the empty breakfast plates cleared away.

Theo paused, taking in the sight of her in a slim-fitting dress of rich blue that enhanced her subtle beauty and intrinsic sexiness. No wonder he'd had trouble concentrating on the call. He wanted to take her straight back to bed.

Since England she'd dominated his thoughts. He had to find a way to combat that. He needed all his faculties to deal not just with the prospect of fatherhood, but the damage to the company and even more urgently, Toula's issues. His stepsister seemed to be recovering well after her breakdown. But she still suffered memory loss of that traumatic night. What would happen when she returned to Athens? She would need all his support. How could he do that with Isla diverting him?

Persuade her into marriage, that was how.

Once he had Isla locked into his plans he could focus on other things again.

Or maybe she'll be a permanent distraction.

It seemed only too likely.

All the more reason to make sure of her as quickly as possible.

That meant bringing forward his plans. The sooner Isla accepted her idea of raising their child alone was unrealistic, the better. This was his child and he had both a right and an obligation to it.

But if she couldn't understand that, she'd soon see that

her relationship with a once famous, now infamous billionaire made her public property. Anonymity was impossible, even if she didn't know it yet. When she did, he'd be here, ready to support her.

She'd need him then.

Was it selfish to look forward to her recognising that? He admired her independence yet on another level it rankled. He was continually distracted by this one intransigent woman, while she seemed unimpressed. Except in bed.

He felt a scalding rush to his groin. There it was again, the familiar hunger. But he couldn't give in to it now when there were other matters to settle.

Theo rubbed his hand around the back of his neck, registering tense muscles. Not just because so much rode on getting Isla to marry him. But because he regretted what would come next. She was a private person and she'd feel the intense media attention like a blow.

Guilt swarmed through him. Her life had changed because of him. From now on she'd be a press target, something he knew from experience was difficult. He thought of Toula's experiences and his heart sank.

Isla would have to run the gauntlet of the press every day simply because they were together. Even if they weren't together and she tried to live a *normal* life away from him there'd be paparazzi following her and their child.

He walked onto the terrace.

Instantly she turned, as if sensing his presence. He liked the way she seemed attuned to him. Maybe it was a residue of last night's intimacy. Would it survive what was to come?

'Your meeting went well?'

'As well as could be expected.' Seeing her raised eyebrows, he went on. 'Business hasn't been straightforward since my arrest. The company is sound but my reputation dived and that had a flow-on effect.'

'Surely with your release that's over, even if Spiro Stavroulis is still pestering you.'

Theo went to take a chair beside her then changed his mind. He thought more clearly with some distance. Instead he closed his hands around the balustrade of the glass railing and looked across the city to the shimmering sea.

'Despite its size, Karalis Enterprises is essentially a family company and has been for generations. The name and the family are at the heart of its success. My father and his father before him were good men, sound in business and honest. The character of the CEO plays a huge part in how the company is viewed. Several major contracts and new investments were scheduled for the last couple of months and now…' Theo shrugged.

'That's so unfair.'

Her chair scraped then Isla was beside him. He felt her gaze, just as he did every time she looked at him. It was something he'd experienced with no one else and made him frown.

'Don't worry, I'm working through it. Things will be well in the long term. I'll still be able to provide for you and our baby.'

She turned away, planting her smaller hands on the balustrade and like him, staring out at the view instead of at him. 'That's not what I meant!'

Theo knew it wasn't but it was easier to focus on what needed to be done, instead of carrying her back to bed, if he kept a little distance between them.

His mouth rucked up in a bitter smile. Who was he kidding? Even when she was annoyed with him he had trouble thinking straight around her.

'Of course not. I know you're not here for my money.' A mirthless laugh escaped. He almost wished she were because then it would be easier to bind her and their child to him and a life in Greece.

'But there's something else I need to speak with you about. Something important.' He dragged his phone from his pocket. 'Last night we were photographed returning from the restaurant.'

'I don't understand.'

Of course she didn't. Isla's life was as sheltered from the press as his had been until his mother married into the Karalis family. Even then Theo hadn't been bothered much until he was working in the company and old enough to feature in those stupid lists of sexiest or wealthiest men.

He found the photo that had started this morning's media furore yet he didn't immediately hand her the phone. Looking into her misty blue eyes Theo felt a pang of regret at how her life changed now because of him. He couldn't prevent that. In fact he was about to escalate it, to get the worst over with as quickly as possible. And show her they needed to be together. Yet part of him wished he could secrete her away in some private paradise and keep her just for himself.

'Theo, what's so bad about a photo?'

He passed the phone to her and watched her eyes grow round.

'But this isn't even a Greek media outlet. This is British.'

'We made the news through Europe, North America, Asia and beyond.'

She bit her lip as she read the speculation about her relationship with the multibillionaire so recently arrested for murder. The piece made him sound dangerous while Isla was portrayed alternatively as an unaware innocent or a gold digger who didn't care about her lover's morals.

'That's libel!' Her horrified face turned to him.

'I suspect they've stayed just this side of libel.'

'What are you going to do? You can't let them print such lies about you.'

Theo blinked then took her hands in his. Her first thought wasn't for her reputation but his. That knowledge was a glowing, precious kernel deep in his chest. Proof that, despite her misgivings, they could move forward to build a strong relationship worthy of their child.

She cares for you.

Just as he'd believed when she visited the prison.

Theo had told himself this was something he could capitalise on to get her to marry. Yet what he felt now had nothing to do with future plans and everything to do with feelings.

'I've got strong shoulders. But if they go too far my legal team will prosecute. For now my focus has to be on mending the damage done to the company.' He paused. 'And keeping you safe.'

He watched her brow pucker as she thought through the situation. Finally, as he'd known she would, she nodded. 'You have a plan, don't you?'

He inclined his head. She'd always been clever and her relative calm in the face of that outrageous piece boded well. Their baby might have thrown him and Isla together but he knew in that moment she wouldn't just be a necessary wife. He suspected she'd be magnificent.

How would it be to share the burdens he carried? To

have someone on his side, apart from his mother, whom he refused to weigh down with more trouble.

'We provide the story they want, but on our terms. The media knows about you now and you won't get any peace until it gets a story. Even then you'll continue to be hounded, especially when your pregnancy becomes news.'

Her hands spasmed in his and he tightened his hold, watching her pupils dilate. It was like watching her innocence being stripped away and it made him feel wrong inside, but he had to go on. She needed the truth.

'Even if you decide not to marry me and opt to bring up our child alone…' As if he'd let that happen! 'The press won't let up. They'll be there whenever you leave your London flat. They'll interview clients at the shop where you work. They'll go through your rubbish to find out what your pregnancy diet is and turn it into some fad diet for their readers or report you're endangering the baby by eating poorly. Later they'll print stories about what you feed our child and if they have no idea, they'll make it up.'

Isla looked so appalled he felt almost guilty spelling it out but she needed to know. 'It's true. The stories they've printed about my stepsister, often without a single word of truth, are legion.' The fact that Toula sometimes behaved erratically hadn't helped.

'They pursued her? I didn't know.'

'Toula has some personal problems but the media loves to portray her as an indulged rich kid, acting out.' Theo paused, reining in anger. He was tempted to explain about his stepsister now but this was enough for Isla to take in at the moment. 'Between their attacks on Toula and on me, I know what to expect. There'll be a media scrum outside any childcare centre you use and as for first day at school—'

'Enough! I get it.'

Reading her distressed expression and pale features he saw she did. He felt the tremor in her hands and vowed to protect her.

'So what's the plan? How do we take back control? And don't say by marrying.'

But they would. Theo was determined on that. Once she understood what he could offer, and how difficult life would be without him at her side, she'd change her mind.

'We dictate the narrative, and we control access to you. I have the resources to provide twenty-four-hour protection wherever you are. It can be so discreet you won't notice it but there will be times when it needs to be up front and obvious to everyone.'

'Bodyguards?' Isla pulled her hands away. 'I'm not sure about that.'

'I am.' Isla was his now, whether she admitted it or not. He couldn't allow anyone to harm her. 'I've lined up an excellent female protection agent.' He read Isla's mutinous look and intervened before she could object. 'She'll be here soon for you to vet. It's important you feel you can trust her.' He waited until finally she nodded. 'And I have plans for our next outing. Next time you're seen it will be in a situation we can control, rather than have photographers mob you in the street.'

It was the casual way Theo mentioned being mobbed in the street that finally convinced Isla. And the pain in his voice when he'd spoken of his stepsister, Toula, being victimised. There'd been something in his voice then that she'd never before heard. A raw ache that made her nape prickle and a slew of questions form on her tongue. But it hadn't been the right time to ask.

So she'd agreed to interview the bodyguard. Fortunately she turned out be someone Isla could imagine spending time with. Of a similar age but with impressive qualifications, she didn't look like a bodyguard and Isla found herself enjoying her understated sense of humour.

That was the first hurdle over. The second was preparing for a gala event Isla would attend with Theo that night. It sounded daunting with formal dress and high-profile attendees. She felt out of place and she hadn't even left the apartment.

Everything had been brought to her here. Racks of amazing designer gowns, shoes in every colour and style, so that even with the help of an expert stylist, choosing what to wear had taken ages. Then there were the masseuse, beautician and hairstylist who spent hours with her.

It was enough to make a woman feel like Cinderella, yet despite the gorgeous clothes and the light but expert makeup that turned her into a sophisticated stranger, it was the massage she loved best. Until then her shoulders had been up near her ears, tension riding her because there was no going back to her old life, even if she wanted to.

But you don't want to, do you? Despite everything you'd rather be here with Theo.

That's what made all this so tough. She fought her own desires when she stood firm against his plan for marriage. It would be easy to agree and be swept along by the juggernaut that was Theo Karalis, the man who made the impossible happen with ease. She could marry him and know her child would grow up with two caring parents. It would know it was loved. How precious was that?

Life would be easier for Isla too. No money worries. She could continue her studies. Into the bargain she'd have a handsome, attentive lover, for she had no illusions that Theo intended a paper marriage. He was far too passionate for that.

All that held her back was the fear she teetered on the brink of falling for him again. Of wanting too much from a man who thought about duty, not love. And when he tired of sex with her? She didn't think she could bear being married to him when he took other lovers.

So what are you going to do?

A sound behind her made her swing around.

'Theo.' Her voice was breathless, but who wouldn't be, faced with the handsomest man she'd ever seen, tall and resplendent in bespoke formal wear, looking at her as if he wanted to eat her up?

Her insides turned to liquid and a hungry pulse throbbed at that aching, empty place between her legs. They'd made love most of the night but today he'd kept his distance after that single kiss and Isla discovered she missed him.

From the strong planes of his face to the imposing width of his shoulders and the blaze of his eyes as he surveyed her, he was gorgeous.

He could be yours if you just say the word.

Isla knew Theo could arrange a sumptuous wedding celebration just as quickly and effectively as he'd organised her move to Athens and everything else if she let him.

She bit her lip, afraid in that moment that she might yield to temptation and say yes.

Because you want him.

It was shaming but true. She had little pride left where he was concerned and she was afraid that the more she had of him the more she'd want.

'I knew you'd look stunning,' he murmured, pacing across the bedroom towards her, 'but still I wasn't prepared.'

Isla blinked as she registered his hoarse voice and the dark glow of desire in his eyes. These weren't just pretty words. Joy so strong it ached had her pressing her hand to her breastbone.

It wasn't fair when Theo said such things to her. When he looked at her that way. How could she be sensible?

'The press will be out in force tonight, but don't worry about them. Just follow my lead and it will all work out okay. I'll look after you.'

With that reminder, Isla's starry-eyed gaze cleared.

Tonight wasn't about *them*, together because he craved her company and wanted her to meet his friends. It was about public expectations and managing the media.

Isla discovered that after all it wasn't hard to be sensible about their relationship.

CHAPTER TWELVE

THEO HELPED ISLA from the limo under a barrage of flashing lights. Voices called his name, shouting questions. He ignored them. All his attention was on the woman whose hand rested in his.

He felt her shudder at the blare of light and noise surrounding them and wanted to shield her.

'Take your time,' he said softly. 'It'll be okay, I promise. All you have to do is walk inside with me. You don't have to say anything.'

He squeezed her hand as their eyes met and his brain blocked out the hubbub. There was just the two of them.

'Trust me, Isla.'

Finally she nodded and stepped from the car, eyes locked on his, and his breath caught. She was magnificent and her being here felt suddenly like the greatest proof of trust and loyalty.

No matter what he told himself about Isla having no escape from press attention now they knew about her, it took guts to throw her lot in publicly with a man whose once vaunted reputation was now stained. She could have refused to come tonight. Instead she'd risen to the challenge.

She straightened and the din around them eased for real as hardened journalists forgot their questions.

Theo knew the feeling. When he'd first seen her tonight his larynx had frozen while other parts of his body clamoured into eager life.

Her hair was up in an elegant style that left a couple of chestnut curls loose to kiss her neck. Strands of twisted gold threaded through her hair, reminding him of a portrait he'd seen of a beautiful woman from classical times. Isla wore gold, a dress of tiny pleats that burst into life under a renewed barrage of lights as the photographers went wild. The full-length gown was modelled on classical lines, with golden cords around her waist and under her bust, the fine fabric moulding her slim body and beautiful breasts, leaving her pale arms and throat bare. Its clinging fit revealed the tiny curve of her belly, but not obviously proclaiming her pregnancy.

She looked like a goddess. *His* goddess.

Theo was torn between pride as he tucked her arm through his and unfamiliar trepidation, as if no mere man had a right to touch this scintillating, celestial being.

Except Isla was warm flesh and blood. He drew her close and felt that tiny shiver of response that she couldn't quite hide. Her gaze clung to his and as the moment lengthened, he saw her anxiety fade as excitement stirred.

He was tempted to hustle her back into the car and then home where they could be alone.

'Should we move?' she breathed.

He blinked and saw they were still beside the limo. The shouts had reached fever pitch. 'Let them have their photos. They'll bother us less later.'

Except they'd probably clamour even harder for photos of this stunning woman.

Then he noticed the goosebumps on her arms and led her forward, keeping her close for warmth but also in unmistakeable possessiveness. He urged her into the prestigious museum and instantly the decibels dropped.

'I should have insisted you wear a coat.'

'And spoil the impact of the dress?' She shook her head. 'It's the only time I've had a chance to wear anything so gorgeous. I wasn't going to hide it. Besides, it's warm enough in here.'

Not surprising as the huge entry space was filled with the great and the good not only of Athens but from across Europe and beyond. The opening of the new wing was a huge event, years in the planning.

Their arrival caused a ripple of reaction. He saw it like a wave on an otherwise still sea, heads turning, conversations breaking off and beginning again in whispers.

Theo should be used to it yet it still angered him that there were people willing to believe the worst, despite proven facts. Even the evidence that proved he wasn't on the stairs where Spiro Stavroulis had died seemed to have little impact.

Theo stood taller, shoulders back. He sensed Isla glance up at him. This time it was her hand squeezing his. He jerked his gaze away from the crowd, surprised to discover what looked like sympathy in hers. He knew she'd been nervous, even annoyed at finding herself in the eye of a media storm. Now she looked at him with an expression that spoke of warmth and understanding.

'Theo! I'm so glad you could make it.'

He turned to see a familiar smiling face. Not only one but several. There were handshakes and warm greetings as he introduced Isla to the museum's director and his wife, to the head of the nation's archaeology service and the government minister who'd got this major expansion funded.

After that the event went smoothly, though Theo had to reiterate his refusal not to make a speech. Karalis money might have contributed substantially to the project but he wasn't in the mood for public addresses, despite what his PR team advised. He was here tonight for Isla, giving her a taste of what she could expect but limiting her exposure to the prying public. He wouldn't leave her alone to take the limelight on the podium.

Theo set himself to circulate, to introduce her to some of the more interesting guests and make the evening easier for her. They'd met politicians and business leaders, socialites and academics and Isla held her own. Even with a sharp-tongued doyenne of Athenian society who he knew still intimidated his mother. He'd been ready to step in, but Isla handled her perfectly with quiet dignity and honesty. She refused to be bullied, instead responding with questions of her own till the old woman laughed and announced she was a refreshing change from the usual thoughtless girls she met. *That* set people gossiping, but in a good way.

Yet Theo sensed the effort it took for Isla to keep her poise. This wasn't her milieu. But when they met a knot of archaeologists and historians she was in her element, listening avidly as they discussed the exhibits.

They were leaving when disaster threatened. The crowd before them parted and there was Stavroulis, eyes blazing retribution.

Theo's instinct was to lead Isla away before the old man launched another venomous attack. But to turn away would be to insult the grieving man and Theo couldn't do that. Despite the hurt he'd inflicted, Stavroulis suffered.

But Theo did pull her protectively against his side as he

approached the other man. The crowd around them hushed and he felt the expectation as a ripple of excitement.

He nodded. 'Stavroulis.' Then he turned. 'Isla, I'd like you to meet Spiro Stavroulis.' When he looked back at the other man it was like looking into a mask, so tightly did he hold in his feelings. 'This is Isla Jacobs, from England.'

Stavroulis's eyes flashed. Would he scream an insult at Theo or storm away without a word? Before he could do either Isla spoke. Not only that but she moved out of Theo's embrace and right up to the old man.

'I heard about your grandson.' The drop of a pin would have been loud in the silence. 'What a terrible thing. I'm so sorry for your loss.'

Theo's heart hammered a staccato beat as he stepped up beside her, muscles tensing, ready to intervene if necessary. He'd visited the man to offer his condolences, only to have them violently spurned. He wouldn't allow Stavroulis to try that with Isla.

But after a pregnant silence during which Theo noticed more than one phone raised to capture the moment, Stavroulis inclined his head in a stiff bow and thanked her. He even added that it was a pleasure to meet her before spinning on his heel and marching away.

Isla was silent on the way home, ignoring the paparazzi and the security team who cleared the way.

No wonder she was preoccupied. The evening hadn't gone as he'd planned. It had backfired, with Isla in the firing line.

'That was awful,' she said as they entered the sitting room, confirming his thoughts.

She shivered and hugged her arms around herself and

Theo hated that he'd been responsible for that. He strode across to get them drinks. She wasn't drinking alcohol but he needed something to do, pouring her a soft drink then a brandy for himself that he knocked back in one swallow. It was sacrilege to treat the fine spirit that way, but he welcomed its burn.

'I apologise. I should have checked if he'd be there tonight. He so rarely goes to such events I didn't consider the possibility that he'd confront us. Are you okay?'

'*Me?* It's *you* I'm thinking of. How dare so many of them treat you like that, when you've done nothing wrong?'

Theo stared, his brain playing catch-up with her words. Isla was annoyed on his behalf?

'As for the way they watched you, and that man…' She shook her head. 'It makes me sick.'

He put the soft drink down and moved closer. 'The nausea is back?' Now he really felt guilty. She'd been doing so well lately.

Isla's gaze meshed with his and heat slammed into him as he felt the full force of her fury. Then she gave a lopsided smile. 'Not literally. But the injustice makes me so angry. Treating you both as if you're some sort of public amusement.'

Theo stared. 'You're angry with the guests?'

'Of course! I know there were plenty who were genuinely glad to see you but there were others who enjoyed the drama at your expense. Even after all you've been through.'

His expense not hers. Something shuddered deep inside as her words touched a part of Theo that he'd kept isolated behind his strongest defences.

He couldn't accustom himself to the fact Isla thought

of him when *she* was the one pregnant and tired, facing the future in a foreign land, complete with paparazzi and gawking socialites. 'It's you I worry about. I'm okay, I've—'

'Got broad shoulders, so you keep saying.' She shook her head. 'But it's still outrageous.'

She fizzed with energy, like a lit firework about to explode. Theo reached out and took her wrists, gently tugging her arms from around her ribs and pulling her to him, trying to calm her restlessness.

'Don't get worked up about it. It's not good for you or the baby. I'm fine.' It took more than a bit of malicious speculation to get the better of him. 'It's *you* I'm concerned about. Stavroulis is a volatile man. I worried how he'd react when you approached him.'

Isla shook her head. 'That poor man. Imagine losing a family member to violence and not knowing who was responsible.'

Theo's jaw clenched on a familiar spasm of regret. The whole situation was appalling. If only Toula had never met Costa Stavroulis. If only the guy hadn't gatecrashed the family party.

If only, if only. Were there any more fruitless words?

'Theo?' He looked down to see her bright eyes fixed on him. 'You look…haunted. Is it from seeing Stavroulis again?'

That was the least of it, but the full story wasn't his to tell. He only had suspicions. How could he act on those, knowing the consequences?

'Don't fret about me,' he growled. He was buffeted by frustration at circumstances he couldn't change and the roiling emotions that surfaced every time he was with Isla, or thought about her.

It wasn't the drama of tonight's scene that ripped at him, but that he'd brought this woman into the heart of it all. It would have been easier for her if he'd let her stay in England, out of the limelight. But how could he have? He needed her with him.

Her and their child.

Except when he looked into those silvery-blue eyes it wasn't her pregnancy he thought of. It was her fire, her determination, her stoicism in the face of so many traumas. Her sympathy and warmth.

How he wanted that warmth, that sympathy now.

'Theo?' She licked her lips and swayed closer.

What did she see in his expression? He'd warned himself to keep his distance because she messed with his head and because he'd already let her down. But the words were already in his mouth.

'I want you, Isla.' His voice was rough with a hunger so deep he'd never experienced its like.

He *needed* her so much it made him shake, because he was selfish and losing himself with Isla was the closest he'd come to finding peace in forever. Not that it was peace he wanted now, but the sheer addictive bliss of melding himself with her. Of finding that place where together they touched heaven.

Theo's chest ached and he realised his breath had stopped. Until Isla leaned in, rising on her toes to brush her lips across his.

The air rushed from his lungs like water from a bursting dam. He gathered her to him, lifting her and covering her mouth with his. A storm of sensation hit as their lips met and clung. There was nothing tentative about their kiss now. It was the full-bodied kiss of lovers too long apart, filled with hunger as well as delight and homecoming.

Isla said something, the sound muffled in his mouth, but Theo recognised it as his name. Just as he recognised acute need in the clamp of her fingers against the back of his skull.

No matter the circumstances that had brought them to this point, they were equals in this.

'I need you now, Theo.'

Theo lifted his head. 'The bedroom. I need to take care of you—'

Her fingertips raked his scalp, sending flashes of lightning into his blood and straight to his groin.

'I don't need that. I'm not going to break. *Now*, Theo.' She sculpted herself against him, her softness fitting perfectly against his unyielding body and in her voice he heard his own desperation.

Fighting the shudders of excitement building deep within, he turned with her in his arms and carried her to the nearest upright surface, resting her back against the wall and hitching her higher as he pressed himself close to support her.

The misty blue of her eyes disappeared in a silvery flash and she gasped as their bodies fitted against each other. Theo felt like molten metal poured through his veins, his lungs were bellows, fanning the blaze she ignited in him.

He gathered the fine fabric of her long dress in his hands, bunching it up till her legs were bare. She lifted one slim leg and he grabbed it, settling it over his hip. Someone groaned as their bodies tilted together, then her other leg settled around his waist and he couldn't help that hard thrust that notched his erection against her pelvis. Even through layers of fabric it felt like bliss.

'I didn't plan this well.' He still wore his trousers but he refused to step back to undo them. No power on earth could drag him away from Isla now.

Her gasp of laughter teased him as she scrabbled at his belt while he dragged down the zip. A few long moments of fumbling that tested him to the limit then he was free, his swollen length hard against her heat. Delicate lace scraped his skin and he shuddered as that took him too close to the edge.

Neither laughed now. Their need was too intense.

Theo's normally deft fingers felt clumsy as he slid them under that lace. Isla was slick and hot, pushing eagerly against his touch, her urgency fanning the lit fuse of his desire.

Fabric tore and even that tiny sound made his flesh tighten with anticipation. Then there was only sensation. Heat surrounded him, Isla's legs pulling him close as he guided himself to her centre.

There. A moment to align himself, to catch his own reflection in her shining eyes and he drove home, long and hard, and his eyes threatened to roll back in his head at how exquisite Isla was.

A shudder went through them both, travelling between their bodies as if they weren't separate entities but one being. Theo hefted a breath that turned into another shudder at the friction of her breasts against his chest. He wanted her naked but that would have to be later. He wanted her in so many ways his brain threatened to overload.

No time for that now. There was only the need, blood deep and raw, between them.

He planted his hand on the wall beside her head for support as he withdrew and thrust again, twisting a little and hearing her cry out in delight as he found just the right spot.

Isla's hands ran over him, her mouth working as if to speak, until he slid his other hand between them to find that swollen jewel at her core and she shouted his name, arching her neck and pressing her head back.

Theo kissed her throat, finding that most sensitive spot at the base of her neck as he stroked her with his hand and his body.

The tremors began inside her, harbingers of a crisis so profound he expected it would destroy them both. But there was no stopping now. He lavished all his skill into feeding the fire, giving Isla everything, all the pleasure she deserved, all of himself.

Nails pricked his skin and her encircling legs tightened. They moved together, so attuned that when the fire burst inside Isla, it seared him too.

She cried out, but as her climax filled her, Isla's diamond-bright eyes held his. As if part of her feared the force of what they'd unleashed.

Theo cupped her cheek, seeking to reassure her. She convulsed around him, milking his very essence, drawing him into herself. Then everything broke apart in pleasure so intense it felt like joy and flame together.

Isla called his name, her voice a feather in the midst of an inferno, but he heard it and responded.

Her name on his tongue tasted like the food of the

gods, so perfect that he recognised with some arcane, inexplicable instinct that this was far more than sex.

What they shared had the power to stop worlds and change lives.

CHAPTER THIRTEEN

ISLA STEPPED OUT onto the roof terrace the next morning to see Theo powering the length of the pool. The sight stopped her in her tracks.

He really was an extraordinarily charismatic man. Even doing laps it was hard to take her eyes off him. The steady rhythm, the play of sunlight across the sleek muscles of his broad shoulders and back, the kick of those powerful thighs…

She pressed a hand to her abdomen where sensation fluttered. It would be nice to think it was her baby moving but she suspected it was simply a response to Theo.

He looked so…elemental in the water, a study in male strength. She recalled all that energy focused on her last night and her breath backed up in her lungs. The phenomenal focus and vigour, the potency of the man. She'd gone from feeling upset on his behalf to needing him with an intensity that surpassed anything she'd known.

That first coupling, barely inside the apartment, had been urgent and extraordinary. As if he'd taken them both to an unfamiliar plane. Afterwards her legs had been boneless and her heart filled with the extraordinary conviction that being with Theo was the one true, right thing in the world.

Later they'd slept until the early hours when they'd come together again, this time slowly, sweetly and his touch as he stroked her body had been almost reverent. It had been exquisite and had left her marvelling, hoping that perhaps things weren't as simple as she thought. Perhaps this wasn't just about their child.

Maybe Theo felt more for her than she'd imagined.

It was true that duty figured in his thinking. But he felt deeply too. Look at the way he'd treated old Mr Stavroulis last night. The man had made himself into an enemy with his quest for vengeance, yet she'd seen Theo's sympathy. She admired him for not shunning the man and hurrying her way. He understood the grief that drove him.

When Theo had spoken of his stepsister too, she'd *felt* his emotion. He genuinely cared for Toula.

Was it too much to hope that perhaps he cared for her as well? Or was it wishful thinking?

She sighed and crossed the terrace towards the pool. If she'd known he was swimming she'd have come straight here instead of having a shower.

With an effort Isla dragged her gaze from Theo, looking at the spectacular view of Athens and the Aegean beyond. Spring had started and soon the warmer weather would be here.

Where would she be then?

She'd planned to be back in London. But did she want that?

Her breath caught in her chest. What she *wanted* was Theo, but not a Theo who viewed her as an obligation or necessary encumbrance. She wanted to be special in her own right. Was it possible that his feelings might grow over time and that his idea of a practical marriage could transform into the love match she'd always wanted?

Last night he'd made her feel special. Maybe—

'Isla!'

Theo surged from the pool in one lithe movement that drew attention to his innate athleticism. He stood tall, flicking the water from his head, his chest rising with each breath after that intense swim.

Isla's mouth dried and a pulse started up between her thighs as she took in the sight of him wearing nothing but dark swim shorts.

Was it any wonder he'd bowled her over when they first met? He looked like a Greek god. She should know, she'd spent long enough studying images of them. But none moved her the way this flawed, flesh-and-blood man did.

'I didn't know where you were,' she blurted out, then wondered if she'd revealed too much.

Theo didn't seem to think so. He marched across and planted a swift but devastating kiss on her mouth. His lips were cold but his mouth warm and he sparked fire in every secret place. Her knees wobbled as he pulled back. 'Sorry, I'm wet.' Honey-gold eyes framed by spiky black lashes mesmerised her then he turned and reached for a towel.

It was only as Theo dried himself that Isla noticed her shirt was damp. Not damp enough to cool her ardour.

He turned back, rubbing his hair so it stood up in tousled crests. He looked almost boyish except for the knowing light in his eyes and the body that belonged to a male in his absolute prime.

'I wanted to wake you.' His voice hit that husky, tantalising note she couldn't resist. 'But thought I should work off some excess energy in the pool first.'

'Did you succeed?'

Theo shook his head. 'There's only one sure-fire remedy for that.' His gaze was a caress, stroking her libido into thrumming life. 'But last night I wasn't gentle. I thought you might be sore.'

Isla lifted her chin. 'If I'd wanted gentle I would have told you. Besides, we went there later.' She'd loved both. The tenderness they'd shared had been as powerful in its own way as the earlier, almost violent surge of need between them.

His smile, a mix of satisfaction and affection, threatened to undo her. But then his expression turned serious. 'Anyway, we need to talk.'

Isla heard strain in his tone. That stopped her impulsive confession that last night had been the most wonderful experience of her life. She still didn't know for sure where she stood with Theo.

'Shall we?' He gestured to some padded sun loungers.

'You don't want to get dressed?' Isla knew how distracting his glorious body would be. If they were discussing something important she needed to concentrate.

'I've spent too much time cooped up inside. I'd rather enjoy the fresh air. There's no cold wind and I'll dry in the sunshine.'

Isla's heart dipped as his explanation took on a darker cast. He wasn't just talking about hours in business meetings. Theo had been incarcerated. Something he didn't speak of except when she'd made it a test of his ability to trust and share with her. Basically she'd blackmailed him.

Her pulse quickened and she blinked back moisture, distressed for all he'd suffered.

'Isla, are you okay?'

'Of course. What did you want to discuss?'

Theo sat beside her but instead of stretching his legs

out, he sat sideways, elbows resting on his knees, facing her. 'It's about my family. Toula and my mother have been away from Athens but my mother just contacted me. She's returning to Athens soon.'

'So I'll get to meet her?' Isla tried to read his expression but failed, as if he deliberately held his feelings in. Did he worry they wouldn't like each other?

She felt that old pang of uncertainty, as if she didn't measure up. It had plagued her through childhood as the girl no one wanted, the girl unworthy of love. Did Theo believe his family would meet her and recognise she was fundamentally lacking?

Isla slammed shut those thoughts. She'd moved beyond such thinking, hadn't she? She had as much right to respect and affection as anyone. It was just the stress of the current situation, throwing up old weaknesses.

'Absolutely. She's already heard about you and is eager to meet you. That's why she's returning.' Theo frowned at his clasped hands.

'You don't want that?' Isla tried not to feel defensive.

Theo shrugged. 'I don't want you feeling pressured. I haven't told her about the baby and I know it's important to you to have time to think things through.'

Relief welled. He was concerned for *her* sake, not because he thought she wasn't good enough for his family.

'I'd like to meet her.' Maybe meeting his family would help Isla with her decision. 'She and Toula have been on holiday together?'

He lifted his head. 'No. My mother's in Corfu with a friend on a short break. It's the first time she's left Athens in months. It took a toll on her, Costa's death, my arrest and all the appalling stories. But she visited me in prison then did what she could to help since my release.'

Isla's heart went out to the woman 'It must have been a trying time for all of you. At least she had Toula with her through the worst of it.'

Theo's mouth twisted. 'Not quite.' Again he paused and it struck her that this assured man was, for the first time to her knowledge, unsure how to proceed.

'It's funny. If you'd been one of those women pursuing me for my money you'd have done your homework and already know at least a version of this from the press.' He saw her stiffen and raised his hand. 'Not that I'm complaining. It's just…difficult, something we don't talk about outside the family.'

Isla jerked back. What was he talking about? She'd known from the news reports that Theo had a sister and widowed mother but her focus had been entirely on his arrest and subsequent release. Maybe the UK press didn't have as much detail about the case either.

'But you *are* family. Even though you haven't agreed to marry me.'

She felt his gaze like a palpable weight, yet this time it didn't feel like a burden, rather like a warm enfolding blanket. Had her feelings altered so much?

'We're linked and always will be, Isla. Whatever happens in our relationship, I want you to know my mother and Toula. They're important to me just as you and our child are.'

She searched for a response but found herself choked up at how he included her with his family. Did he have any idea how appealing that was?

'Sorry, I'm so used to protecting them that this is hard to discuss.' He shook his head. 'Toula wasn't vacationing. She had a severe breakdown and has been in a medical facility since the night of the party when Costa Stavroulis died.'

'Oh, Theo!' Isla rose and sat beside him, reaching for his hand. Despite the heat he always generated, his flesh was chilled.

She grabbed the huge towel he'd discarded and wrapped it around his shoulders. 'Let's go inside where it's warm and you can tell me there.'

His mouth curled up in one corner and her predictable heart skipped a beat at that tiny, enticing smile. 'Even my mother doesn't fuss any more about me catching cold.'

Isla hated seeing him so strained. It wasn't the chill air that affected him but worry for his stepsister. 'See, more proof that I wouldn't make a suitable wife.'

'On the contrary. I like it.'

Safer to ignore that, and the stir of excitement his words evoked. 'You must have been frantic, locked up and not able to go to Toula.'

Theo nodded. 'Prison was already a nightmare but that almost undid me. Not being able to support the people important to me.' His fingers closed around hers, gently squeezing, and Isla could almost believe he included her in that group. His next words made her wonder even more. 'I had to stay close to home when I was released, because Toula needed me.'

Yet he'd trekked to London for a business meeting. That didn't quite ring true but before she could ponder it he spoke again.

'All being well, Toula will come back in a month or so and I wanted to prepare you for meeting her, so you understand that she's fragile.'

'She may prefer not to meet me.'

'She's going to be an aunt. Of course she'll want to

meet you! She'll be thrilled that we have something positive to celebrate.' He paused then plunged on. 'My stepsister suffers from depression. She had a difficult childhood and very little stability. My father didn't even know she existed until her mother died, six years ago, not long before his own death.'

'Her mother kept Toula secret from him?'

Even when she'd despised Theo, Isla had tried to tell him about his child. The thought of keeping such a thing secret—

'She did, and seeing the damage she did to Toula...' He shook his head. 'It made me even more determined to help raise our child.'

His blazing scrutiny scorched but Isla didn't turn away. She'd learned to respect his resolve to be a hands-on father.

'What happened?'

'Toula's mother was a singer and very beautiful. She knew my father, my stepfather that is, before he met my mother. The pair had a brief affair then she left the country. From what I've heard, I suspect Toula's mother wasn't even sure of her paternity. She loved excitement, new places and male attention but wasn't good at maternal responsibility.'

His shoulders dropped on a silent sigh. 'Toula had a difficult time, always on the move, but I suspect the real problem was her mother's unreliable parenting. Plus she had male friends on high rotation and some of them shouldn't have been around a vulnerable girl.'

Isla's chest tightened. She understood the dangers for vulnerable children. Some of the kids she'd known had suffered greatly.

'Poor Toula.'

Theo inclined his head. 'She's got a good heart but she finds somethings difficult. When she came to us she was very volatile and hid a lack of confidence with brashness and acting out. It took her some time to believe that we really cared. Then our father died and that was especially tough as they'd just begun to build a special relationship.'

It must have been tough for Theo too but Isla simply nodded.

'She was doing really well until she met Costa Stavroulis.' He scowled. 'He was handsome and charming but quick-tempered and self-indulgent, partying to excess and dragging her with him. It was the worst possible environment. Alcohol and drugs didn't help her mental state and nor did his domineering ways. He went out of his way to undermine her so she was reliant on him. Finally she accepted she didn't like the place she was in and tried to pull back so she could get help. That's when he became aggressive. He wanted her back.'

Isla's stomach hollowed. It was such a sad, familiar story. 'I'm guessing she didn't invite him to the party?'

'She told him she didn't want to see him again plus I'd warned him off, which is one of the reasons I was suspected of assaulting him. Toula was determined to dry out and get her life on track. But he gatecrashed, getting past security when some friends staged a diversion. He was out of control, high on something and aggressive.'

Theo turned to stare across the city. 'He got into an argument with someone and paid with his life. Toula was one of the first to see him lying there and I can still hear the sound of her screams. They just went on and on.' Isla threaded her fingers through his and leaned closer. 'After that she just closed in on herself. She couldn't function, couldn't even talk. She's been in treatment ever since.

The one mercy is that her memory of that night is blank, totally erased.'

'Oh, Theo.' Isla turned and hugged him close. How much he and his family had been through. 'I promise I'll be careful with Toula and take our relationship at her pace. I certainly won't press her to become best friends.'

Molten gold showed in his remarkable eyes as he embraced her and lifted her onto his lap. 'Toula's just as likely to insist that you do.' He paused. 'Sorry, now you're damp.' But his arms stayed firm around her, just where she wanted them.

'I don't care about that.' She sounded choked up and didn't care.

'I'm sorry for upsetting you too.'

As if he were to blame for that horrible series of events. 'It's just pregnancy hormones. I'm fine. You don't need to worry about me.'

'But I do, Isla. All the time.'

It wasn't fair that he affected her this way, his tenderness undoing her resolve to keep her distance. Her heart hammered as she heard herself say, 'I've been thinking. About your invitation to stay here.'

Theo stiffened and she saw excitement in his expression.

'I'm not saying I want to marry you.' Though to her consternation just saying the word made her heart tremble with something she could only describe as joy. 'But I'd like to stay in Athens longer. We need to decide about the future and the best way to do that is if we learn to trust each other.'

She realised she'd been the one throwing up barriers. Theo was the one letting her into his life, giving her access to everything that mattered to him. He was serious about making their relationship work. That humbled her, especially since the reason she tried to hold back emotionally wasn't because she feared Theo but herself.

'You don't trust me yet?'

Isla was silent, searching for the right words. This was momentous and she needed to be absolutely honest but not raise impossible expectations. 'I trust you, Theo. I trust you with my body, my well-being, and I know you wouldn't deliberately hurt me.'

'Of course not, I—'

She stopped his words with her fingertips against his lips. 'And I trust you to do your best for our baby. I know you'll be a terrific father.' Whenever she thought of it there was a warm glow in her belly. She knew Theo would be strong but tender and encouraging. 'But that doesn't mean we need to marry. I still have reservations. I need to think through the implications.'

Because she knew now, more than ever, that Theo had the power to hurt her as no one else had. She'd thought parting from him the first time was tough but if she married him it would be because she loved him, even if she didn't say the words. She didn't think she had the capacity to pick up the pieces if he shattered her heart again.

Theo's embrace was gentle as he held her to him. 'You're telling me to be patient.'

Isla felt his broad chest rise and fall against her on a deep breath. What argument would he use next?

Finally he nodded. 'This courtship is going to be excellent for my character.' He bent his head and she caught a twinkle in his eyes. 'But we can enjoy ourselves while I'm being patient, can't we?'

He nuzzled the sensitive skin below her ear then grazed his teeth there, making her shiver.

'Absolutely.'

'Excellent.'

His hand went to the top button of her shirt as his mouth closed over hers and Isla found herself forgetting what it was that had so worried her. When Theo seduced her she felt…cherished. Could it be that she was fretting over phantoms and this would work out after all?

CHAPTER FOURTEEN

AUTOMATIC GATES SLID open and Theo drove in through a surprisingly lush garden and up to a beautiful two-storey home with shutters framing long windows and soft terracotta tiles on the roof. In the turning circle before the door a delicate fountain tinkled soothingly as he switched off the engine.

Isla slid damp hands down her trousers, taking in the elegant charm of the property. Nerves danced down her spine.

'You'll be fine.' Theo squeezed her hand then kissed it. 'She's not scary, just excited. I've never brought a woman home to meet the family before.'

'You've never…!'

His eyes crinkled as he got out of the car and she knew he'd waited to drop that bombshell, knowing it would distract her. Then suddenly they weren't alone. A handsome woman in red hurried towards the car. 'Theo, Isla, you're here at last.'

'Mamma.' Theo bent down to envelop her in a bear hug. Then he turned and reached for Isla's hand. 'I'd like you to meet—'

'Isla. I'm so pleased to see you.' The older woman's

voice and brown eyes were warm as she shook Isla's hand. 'It's so kind of you to visit.'

From what Theo had told her Isla had expected a strong-minded woman, kind but a little daunting. She was surprised to feel the other woman's hand tremble as if she too were nervous.

'It's lovely of you to invite me. I don't know anyone in Athens yet, other than Theo.'

Mrs Karalis shook her head. 'We'll remedy that.' Then she leaned in and embraced her warmly. 'Now, that's a better welcome.' Her eyes sparkled and her smile was vivacious as she linked Isla's hand through her arm. 'Come inside, we have so much to talk about.'

And they did. Isla hadn't thought herself particularly loquacious, but that afternoon was full of laughter and conversation. Instead of the interrogation she'd expected they chatted nonstop and easily. Isla felt like she'd been accepted into a circle of warmth and belonging.

At one point Mrs Karalis sent Theo to check the charcoal burner outside while she led Isla into the kitchen.

'Men love to play at being chefs. Give them a fire and something to cook on a skewer and they're happy.' She lifted the lid on a simmering dish and Isla's nose twitched.

'That smells wonderful.'

'It's my beef *stifado*.' She paused then shrugged. 'In the old days we couldn't afford meat often. This was a high treat. It's one of Theo's favourites so I hope you like it.'

'If it tastes like it smells, I'm sure I will.'

'He's…well? He doesn't tell me much, because he doesn't like to worry me, but these last months have been difficult for him.'

Isla met serious brown eyes and saw a depth of affection and worry that made her heart twist.

'He's well.' She stifled the memory of two nights when Theo had tossed and turned, rubbing the scar on his temple and muttering beneath his breath, obviously having a bad dream. Once he'd even shouted out, until she'd whispered soothing words and he'd subsided back into quiet sleep. She barely knew his mother but didn't want to worry her. She and her family had already been through so much. 'He's busy with the company though and concerned about you and his sister.'

'He told you about Toula?' The other woman's head came up.

'A little. That she hadn't been well and was recuperating.'

Mrs Karalis nodded. 'She's had some difficulties and taking up with Costas Stavroulis was disastrous for her. But I believe she's turned a corner. With luck…'

Theo came in then, saying the first course was ready.

The rest of the day the three of them were together, talking, laughing and eating. There were no more confidences but by the time they left Theo's mother had already arranged a date for her and Isla to meet for lunch and visit her favourite knitting shop. And when they parted the older woman's hug was even warmer than before.

It was early days but Isla couldn't help but imagine what it would be like to be a permanent part of this small, deeply caring family. If she married Theo she and their child would *belong*. It was a heady thought.

Theo's chest was aflame. Each breath felt like burning coals dragged over raw flesh. But the physical pain didn't matter. It was the horror of being here, in this tiny dark place, so small he couldn't even stand. The walls and ceiling were shrinking around him and soon he'd hear his bones crack as he was pulverised into dust.

He shoved the metal door with all his strength, despite knowing it was useless. He'd keep trying until his final breath. He had to get out of here because—he felt the hair rise on his nape—Isla was in the cell next to him. She didn't cry out, she was too stoic for that, but he *knew* she was there. He sensed it in every aching atom of his body. In the terrible thud of his heart against his ribs.

A scream rent the air, high-pitched with fear. Toula.

Theo scrabbled at the door, fingers bleeding. He hammered his shoulder against it. He couldn't let harm come to them. Not Isla. Not—

'Theo!' Isla's voice came, cool running water against his burning body. He gasped, pain searing his chest. 'Open your eyes, Theo.'

Slender fingers shaped his face but he couldn't be distracted. He needed to save—

'Please, Theo.'

Something soft brushed his face and the scent of rosemary filled his nostrils. Rosemary and sweet woman.

He snapped his eyes open. 'Isla!'

'It's all right, Theo. You're safe.'

'You're here.' In the darkness he reached for her, gathering her to his pounding chest, wrapping his arms, his whole body around her, rocking her close. 'You're safe.'

'Of course I'm safe. We both are. You had a nightmare.'

Theo exhaled, his body shuddering with relief. A nightmare. He had them occasionally but usually he managed not to wake Isla.

He swallowed, his throat scratchy. Had he been calling out? What else had he done? 'Did I hurt you?'

'No, I'm fine. I was just worried about you.'

But Theo ran shaking fingers over her, needing to check, discovering silky skin and fragrant curves. The swell where she carried their child. His heart somersaulted. Safe. Isla and the baby were safe.

'I'm sorry. I didn't mean to scare you.'

'You didn't scare me. But you were so distressed I was concerned.'

She moved as if to reach the bedside lamp but he stopped her, capturing her hand and bringing it to his lips. 'It was just a dream.'

Though his body felt racked with pain from the tension and his belly roiled with remembered fear for Isla and his stepsister.

'They're getting worse, aren't they?'

He stiffened. She *knew* about his dreams? He'd thought he'd concealed them.

When she spoke her voice was soft with a mixture of tenderness and amusement. 'We've shared this bed for almost two months, Theo. It's a very big bed but we always seem to end up in each other's arms. You've been having occasional bad dreams ever since I got here.'

'You never said anything.'

'Nor did you. I thought that, if you wanted to share what's bothering you, you would.'

Theo froze in the act of sliding his fingers through her soft hair. 'There's nothing bothering me.'

Sourness filled his mouth. He hated lying to Isla. But this wasn't his secret to share, no matter that he wanted to. Besides, he only had suspicions that it had been Toula at the top of the stairs that night. Little Toula facing her aggressive ex. She couldn't recall that night at all.

He squeezed his eyes shut, the familiar maelstrom of emotions whirling inside him, so fast he felt light-headed. But what could he do? He couldn't force the issue. He had a duty to protect.

'So it's just the memory of your time in prison bothering you? Nothing else?'

'Isn't that enough?'

Isla stiffened in his hold. She didn't move away yet he sensed her mental withdrawal and silently cursed.

'Of course it is. I think you should see someone, a counsellor, especially as the dreams are getting worse.'

'It's okay. Nothing to worry about.'

Isla said nothing for the longest time and he found himself holding his breath as if awaiting judgement. So many barriers had fallen between them. In every way except Isla's continued refusal to marry, he felt they'd reached a new level of understanding and trust. A trust he broke by not being up-front with her.

But how could he, when it meant a different betrayal? Yet keeping this secret was increasingly hard.

'It's natural the experience would impact on you, Theo.' Her voice was gentle, making him feel even more guilty that he held back one final nugget of truth. 'It doesn't mean you're any less macho.'

Relief stirred. Isla thought his reticence was male ego. That was as good an excuse as any.

'If you don't want to talk about that, there's something else I need to understand.'

'Go on,' he said warily.

'You know I've been seeing Simon at the University?'

'Of course.'

His friend was trying to persuade Isla to continue her studies in Athens. In the meantime he'd offered her some part-time work cataloguing finds and doing a little research. Theo had high hopes that soon she'd accept the inevitable, agreeing to marry him and build a permanent life in Greece. They were good together, more than good. Their relationship was better, stronger and deeper than before, unlike any he'd had or could imagine having with any other woman.

She'd even coped amazingly with the media stampede when they announced her pregnancy. His mother and Isla were firm friends and since Toula's recent return the three had bonded in a way he'd hardly dared hope for.

'Today Simon said something that made it clear he hadn't asked that you check on me in London.' She paused. 'That's what you told me.'

Theo released an easy breath. Was that all? Strange how, at the time, it had seemed vital that Isla believe he'd only looked her up as a favour to a friend. His pride wouldn't let him admit the truth, in case she really had washed her hands of him. At the time he'd convinced himself it was best if he sever their relationship, but he hadn't been able to stay away. They'd moved on so far from that.

He shifted onto his back, pulling her closer into his embrace, her head resting at his collarbone, her rounded belly solid against him. He smiled.

'I was protecting myself.'

'From what?' Her hand spread on his ribs and he covered it with his.

'From the likelihood you hated me for cutting you loose.'

Isla's fingers twitched beneath his. 'Well, that was

honest. You're saying you didn't want to admit you wanted to see me but used your friend as an excuse?'

'Put like that it sounds juvenile, doesn't it?' But there hadn't been anything childish about Theo's feelings. 'I believed it for the best that we parted. But even believing that, I kept thinking about you. I couldn't leave it the way I had. I told myself that if I saw you for myself, saw that you'd moved on with your life…'

Even that implied a lie. Isla had become important to him in a short time. He'd told himself in prison it was sentiment and the memory of great sex that kept him thinking of her, but he'd known at a deep, never admitted level it was more than that. He'd needed to see Isla because he felt things for her he'd never experienced before. He wanted her in his life forever and couldn't imagine it without her.

'You wanted to check I was okay so you needn't feel guilty about pushing me away?' Her voice was flat.

'It was more complex than that.' Theo swallowed. 'I cared for you, Isla. I still do, even more so now. When Simon mentioned he'd heard you'd dropped out and your tutor thought you were sick I had to see for myself.'

'Then, when you discovered I had morning sickness, your sense of responsibility kicked in so you couldn't just leave.'

Theo wished he'd let her turn the light on. He wanted to see her face for her tone made him think she was upset. What was wrong with him feeling responsible for her? He'd thought she'd be happy at his admission he'd visited because he cared about her.

'So the sixty-four-million-dollar question is, why did you push me away in the first place? You never gave me a proper explanation.'

Theo hated the brittle edge to her usually warm voice and the tension he felt in her even as she lay naked against him.

'I'm sorry, Isla. I never wanted to hurt you.' He heard her swift intake of breath and continued. 'But I knew you'd be hurt. The way I ended our relationship wasn't ideal.'

'It was brutal.'

'Yes.' He paused. 'I was in a brutal place at the time.' He didn't have words to describe how terrible it had been, not just living in a cell, but the nightmare of it all, help-less to care for those who needed him.

'I'm sorry, Theo.' Warm lips pressed against his col-larbone. 'What I went through was nothing compared with what you suffered.'

'Ah, Isla. Don't apologise. I treated you badly even if it was for the best reasons.'

'Tell me.' She lay her head against him again and he felt the change in her, no longer taut with hurt but sup-ple and receptive.

'I was trying to protect you.'

She made a sound in the back of her throat, somewhere been a laugh and a snort of derision. 'And I was trying to support *you*. You were the one locked up!'

'And I appreciated it. Many so-called friends melted away once the news of my arrest broke.' Fortunately his real friends hadn't. 'It meant a lot, knowing you believed in me.'

She snuggled closer. 'I'm glad. At the time it didn't seem like it.'

Guilt punched him. 'I was brutal because I had to be. You kept turning up at the prison and it wasn't a place for you.' The thought of Isla, even in the waiting room of such a place, made him sick. 'I *had* to send you away.'

Silence. Didn't she believe him? But then he'd never fully shared this with her. His arms tightened, cradling her, his hand stroking her thick hair.

'I felt tainted,' he admitted at last. 'And I wanted to protect you from that.'

'Theo!' He heard her outrage but ignored it.

'My world caved in the day they arrested me, Isla. I truly hadn't believed it possible they'd do such a thing and I wanted you well clear. I didn't want you embroiled in something so sordid, especially when I wasn't free to protect you. You've seen how fascinated the media is by you. Imagine what it would have been like if they'd learned you were my lover.'

He felt her shudder and knew that at last she began to understand. 'It wasn't just the almighty scandal. There was a dangerous edge to it with emotions running high and Stavroulis whipping up so much negativity. I feared for you. It even seemed possible the old man might take out his hatred on those closest to me.'

Before he hadn't intended to share that with her, but he hated keeping things from her.

'Oh, Theo.' She shook her head, her hair brushing his skin.

'I didn't know how long it would take to clear my name. *If ever.* The authorities seemed unwilling to believe the evidence in my favour.' For a while he'd feared he'd never be free. That still haunted his dreams. 'I couldn't allow you to stay in Greece, vulnerable to all that hatred.'

'You pushed me away because you cared?' Her voice was small, as if he'd taken her by surprise.

'Of course. Even when I was released I couldn't go

to you. My mother and Toula needed me badly. I had to stay in Athens to support them. Toula was so fragile…'

Yet that had eaten at him. For the first time family obligation had grated, because it had prevented him going to Isla. He'd been falling for her, he realised with a quiver of recognition. He'd been enchanted by her, charmed, and hadn't understood the depth of his feelings until he'd pushed her away.

No wonder he'd felt empty without her. She'd never been simply a romantic fling, had she? Even before her pregnancy, Isla had been important. She…

'I wish you'd explained all that earlier.'

'If I'd explained, would you have done what I wanted and left Greece?'

'Probably not.'

Of course she wouldn't. His woman was brave if reckless.

His woman.

Theo breathed deep, drawing in the truth of that to his very core. Isla *was* his woman. He felt it in his bones, in his head and his gut. He wanted to say it out loud, make her agree. But he couldn't push her. He had to work for it. How was it that he knew, with every atom of his being, that they were meant to be together and Isla still couldn't see it?

Despite the growing understanding between them, she still held back, refusing to accept marriage. It drove him crazy. What more did he need to do to convince her? He could seduce her into agreement. But was that coercion? Besides, he wanted her thinking clearly and actively deciding to be his wife.

Every time they discussed marriage Isla withdrew, countering every point with some pragmatic, if negligible argument. He had to prove to her that on a practical level it was the most sensible option for them and their child.

'You're a stubborn woman, Isla.'

He felt her smile against his flesh. 'Just as well, since you're the most determined man I know.'

She made it sound like a compliment. 'That's all? Determined?' He moved his hands across her delectable body, slowing as he reached places that made her soften and sigh.

'And sexy,' she sighed, twisting and arching into his touch, her voice suddenly breathless. 'Sexy and sinful.'

Theo nearly told her there was nothing sinful about making love to the only woman he'd ever need. The woman who, he'd discovered, made him whole. But he didn't want to scare her. He'd take it slow, convincing her with his actions and his loving that he was the man for her. Soon, surely, she'd admit it.

He just had to be patient. If it didn't kill him first.

CHAPTER FIFTEEN

'I LIKE THE SWIMSUIT,' Toula said, looking up from her magazine as Isla walked across the roof terrace to the pool, the pavers warm beneath her bare feet. 'I'm glad I persuaded you to buy it. Theo will approve, it's classy but seductive and we all know how sexy he finds you.'

Isla blushed. She'd never had a sister, or anyone really, to talk with frankly about her private life. It took some getting used to but she liked it. She valued her budding friendship with Toula. Theo's mother and stepsister had been so welcoming Isla began to believe she'd found the acceptance, the family, she'd always wanted.

She also adored that Theo found her sexy, even with her now well-rounded curves of obvious pregnancy. Intimacy was more satisfying than ever and even when they weren't making love he usually had his arm around her or her hand in his as if, like her, he felt their growing connection.

'No need to look embarrassed, Isla. It's sweet the way you dote on each other. That's why I always call before coming upstairs to the penthouse, to give you notice.'

Toula's laugh was a rare, lovely sound, making Isla smile.

'I approve. You're good together.' Toula paused, suddenly earnest. Theo's sister was so different to the waif-like woman she'd met weeks ago. More outgoing, more ready to talk. 'He's a good man, you know.'

Isla sank onto a sun lounge next to Toula's. 'I know. He's special.'

She'd seen him with his family and others, both relaxed and under stress. She'd felt his care for her and seen the long hours he worked to get the family business back on track. He was dependable, honest and caring.

They were good together, their trust and affection growing daily. Was it any wonder her doubts disintegrated like water evaporating in the spring sunshine?

Her blood pumped faster. She trusted Theo.

She loved him.

Isla had fought against his logic and her own desires too long. She loved him so much and believed in time he'd learn to love her too. She wanted to be with him and support him.

She was ready to marry him.

'Why don't you put him out of his misery and marry him?'

Isla lifted her head sharply. 'I needed to be sure.'

Toula leaned forward, her magazine falling. 'But you're sure now?'

'That's a discussion for me to have with your brother.'

Eagerness filled her. Maybe tonight before they went out to the black-tie dinner. She'd wear the gold dress he liked so much and tell him her decision. Maybe they'd stay home to celebrate…

Seeing Toula's assessing look, Isla sought a distraction. She glanced at the magazine on the ground and saw it was a university prospectus. 'You're considering study?'

'Perhaps. I don't have a good track record for sticking at things.' Toula shrugged. 'But after all my counselling sessions I've discovered an interest in psychology.'

It was wonderful that Toula was thinking about the future. 'It's not the end of the world if you begin and change your mind. But my experience is that if you find the subject interesting you want to stick at it.'

'You really think I could do it?'

'I don't see why not.'

'Everything is turning out well, isn't it?' Toula gave her a tentative smile. 'I'm feeling better, mamma is happy, Theo has you and he's clearly thriving.'

Isla frowned. 'Well…'

'What?' Isla shifted on the seat, wishing she'd stayed silent. 'Isla? What's wrong?'

Isla bit her lip. She didn't like to dampen Toula's enthusiasm but she knew there was something very wrong, something Theo refused to discuss. But she loved him. Didn't that include an obligation to care for him, despite his belief that he could shoulder every burden?

'Theo is okay,' she said slowly, not wanting to spook Toula. She had her suspicions about the root cause of Theo's trouble but couldn't be sure. 'But he has things on his mind. You should talk to him.'

'You think my brother will open up about something on his mind? He'll clam up. He sees it as his role to protect *me*, though I'm stronger than he thinks.'

Was she? Isla was torn between wanting to see Theo unburdened and caution about Toula's capacity to deal with harsh reality.

'Isla?' Toula's voice was sharp. 'What is it? Tell me.'

She sighed. 'He's had nightmares since prison and they're getting worse.' She met Toula's eyes. 'Do you know some people still think he killed Costa Stavroulis? They gossip about him when he enters a room and it's affected the company's reputation. That's why he works such long hours. Old Mr Stavroulis is making his life hell because he's got no one else to blame.'

Toula paled. 'I had no idea. No one said anything.'

Of course not. Because they worried about her. 'Are you okay, Toula? Maybe I shouldn't have—'

'Of course you should have told me. Mamma and Theo wrap me in cotton wool.' With good reason. But the woman looking back at Isla didn't look panicked. 'Thanks for trusting me with the truth, Isla. It means a lot.'

Isla nodded and hoped she'd done the right thing.

That evening Isla was nervous as she dressed for the reception. Tonight would be special and the Grecian dress gave her confidence. She'd added the gold earrings Theo had given her, beautiful replicas of ancient designs featuring bees feeding from delicate flowers. He'd grumbled about wanting to put a ring on her finger instead but had been mollified at her delight in the gift, precious not just for its monetary value but his thoughtfulness in choosing a design she loved.

It wasn't the reception making her nervous. It was telling Theo she'd marry him, though he didn't love her. Yet. Surely he would one day.

Isla smoothed her hand down her rounded belly and felt the flutter of the baby moving. Anxiety eased as love squeezed her heart. It would be okay. Everything she'd ever wanted was here. A family. A man who lit up her world.

She imagined his delight when she told him. He'd—

The bedroom door swung open and thudded against the wall.

Her heart leapt into her throat. 'Theo?'

Something was wrong. He looked frayed around the edges, something she'd never seen. Usually nothing fazed him. Isla hurried forward as he closed the door carefully. But she stopped as she read his narrowed gaze. She blinked, disbelieving, as she met a furious stare.

'What did you think you were doing?'

'Sorry?'

He shook his head as if trying to clear it. 'Bothering Toula with all that stuff. You *know* how fragile she is.'

Isla's fingers threaded together. 'What's happened? How is she?' Toula had seemed fine, if a bit quiet, when they'd parted two hours ago.

He pinched the bridge of his nose. 'How do you think she is, after you worried her unnecessarily?'

'Theo, is she okay? Does she need someone to be with her?'

'If she does it won't be *you*!' he growled.

Isla stiffened and blinked at his savage tone. 'Tell me, Theo. Does she need company?'

'Apparently not,' he huffed finally. 'We talked in her apartment then she told me to leave because she had things to do.'

Isla took a slow breath. 'Perhaps you should trust Toula to know what's best for her.'

'What would you know about it? You've only known her a short time and suddenly you're an expert?' His chest rose on a mighty breath. 'How *dare* you get her worked up with some sob story about me suffering? And about old man Stavroulis? Were you trying to push her to the edge all over again?'

Isla retreated a step, her hand to her throat, stunned he could say such a thing. He couldn't mean that. It was stress talking. Theo worried about his stepsister, with reason. But Toula's behaviour after their discussion had convinced Isla she'd done the right thing.

'I only—'

'There's no *only* about it. You had *no right*! You don't know what you're stirring up. I don't want you going near Toula or interfering with my family. Keep out of it.'

Her breath was a shocked hiss as his words sank into silence. Ice settled around her heart.

'Yet you want me to marry you and be part of that family.'

'That's not the same thing. That's different.' Theo raked his hand through his hair and turned to pace.

Of course it's different. It was all about the baby.

Isla felt herself crumble inside. All those hopes, all her confidence. A single instant had revealed a truth she'd deliberately avoided facing.

Yet still Isla waited for Theo to apologise, say he didn't mean it.

And waited.

Slowly, reluctantly, she absorbed the truth. Their relationship wasn't real. It was a farce. There was just Theo and his almighty sense of duty, sweetened by physical desire. She'd kidded herself thinking he wanted *her*, spinning fantasies all over again. He wanted their child but she, Isla, was additional baggage.

She'd never *really* belong in that intimate circle he truly cared for. Even if they married she wouldn't belong. She was an outsider and always would be. Second-best. Not worthy of love. Not an equal in his eyes.

Pain lanced her chest and stole her breath.

Isla took a step back and sank onto the bed, knees trembling. How could she have believed there was anything else between them?

Theo stopped pacing near the door as if he couldn't bear to be close to her. 'You've got no idea what you've done. How could you?' His jaw set in a grim line. 'But I can't let you meddle.'

She swallowed a knot of despair and dammed tears. She couldn't get her voice to work so nodded instead.

Theo frowned then stepped forward but she couldn't bear any more. With a sudden, desperate surge of energy she shot to her feet and into the bathroom, locking the door behind her.

Her breaths sounded like sobs as she leaned against the door, scared he'd try to follow. The one thing she had left was pride and she didn't want him to see her undone.

She needn't have worried. Theo didn't follow. Instead she heard a phone ring, then his deep voice, then silence.

How long she stayed there, frozen with distress and misery, she didn't know, but suddenly she felt claustrophobic. She needed air and space to think. Not on the roof terrace where Theo might see her, but out. She had to get out.

Isla didn't remember leaving the apartment or taking the lift. She marched across the marble foyer of the apartment block, catching a flurry of movement from the corner of her eye. Her bodyguard, hurrying to follow.

Isla didn't want company. She needed to be alone.

She picked up her long skirt and hurried onto the street. She'd get a taxi, find somewhere to be alone. In a couple of strides she crossed the pavement, wishing she was wearing flats instead of spindly high heels. Searching the traffic, she stepped onto the street when her heel caught something and out of nowhere the ground came up to meet her.

There was a surge of pain and everything went blank.

CHAPTER SIXTEEN

ISLA'S MOUTH WAS dry and tasted strange. She didn't want to open her eyes. She had a terrible sense of foreboding.

Where was she? Something told her she wasn't in her own bed. She opened her eyes then closed them against the light. Gingerly she reached an arm across the sheet. Her shoulder felt stiff…

'You're awake! Oh, my dear, I'm so happy.' The woman's voice was familiar but Isla couldn't place it. 'Theo will be so relieved. He's been frantic.'

Theo! Theo Karalis.

Isla didn't hear the rest of the words as memory hit like a bombshell. His fury. The revelation of how he really felt about her. Her flight from his apartment. The baby—

Her baby…

Scalding tears leaked from her eyes.

'Please, my baby…' Isla dragged her heavy arm to her abdomen. It was still swollen as if with pregnancy but did that mean anything? There was no fluttery movement inside.

She snapped her eyes open, wincing in the glare, and saw Theo's mother rise from a chair near the bed as a nurse entered.

Isla was in hospital. She tried to catch a breath, telling herself they'd look after her baby. But what if…?

The nurse said something she didn't catch and, with a long backwards look, Mrs Karalis left the room.

'It's good to see you awake, Ms Jacobs.' The nurse took her pulse. 'You probably feel strange but you're safe.'

'My baby?'

Did she imagine a slight hesitation? 'You're still pregnant, Ms Jacobs.'

Isla's breath shuddered in a sigh of relief, her eyes closing as tears streamed down her cheeks. The nurse talked about bruising and X-rays but she didn't take it in. Not until she heard that name again and her heart squeezed.

'Mr Karalis has been here all the time. He's only just left but I'm sure he'll be back any minute.'

'No!' Isla opened her eyes and met the nurse's gaze. 'I don't want to see him. Please. I don't want to see anyone.'

Calm brown eyes surveyed her. 'If that's what you want. Now, let me check you over.'

Isla lost track of time in hospital. Was this only the second night here? There'd been more tests and more reassurances. The baby was fine, they said, though Isla fretted when she couldn't feel it move until they used a monitor so she could hear its heartbeat. She cried again then. She cried a lot, as if she'd saved a lifetime's tears and was only now releasing them.

As for her, bruising they said, and a knock to the head that had initially concerned them. But today the consensus was more cheerful. She could leave soon, though she'd have to have someone with her.

That's what kept her from sleep this evening. She'd be released but where would she go? The staff had passed on a message from Theo's mother, inviting Isla to stay with her, but how could she accept?

Wearily, Isla closed her eyes, telling herself it was better for the baby if she slept now and worried tomorrow.

The door opened and footsteps approached. 'Isla.'

Her eyes sprang open. How had he got in? He must have evaded the staff. She opened her mouth to order Theo from the room then stopped, frowning.

He looked like a stranger, gaunt and dishevelled, dark circles under his eyes, that jagged scar livid and grim lines around his mouth. Isla told herself it was an illusion. He couldn't have lost weight in a couple of days and as for dishevelled, his clothes were of finest quality, made for him. Yet he looked haggard, worse than when he'd woken from nightmare.

'I had to see you. To check myself that you were all right.'

'Don't you mean the check on the baby?'

He flinched but didn't deny it. 'Both of you.' Isla was about to challenge that but his words stopped her. 'I love our child already but I don't know it yet, not like I know *you*, Isla. *You're* the one I'm most afraid of losing. I couldn't bear that.'

'Stop that!' Isla pushed herself up against the pillows as he approached. 'Don't lie to me, Theo.'

He shook his head, eyes never leaving hers as he put his hand his heart. 'No lie, Isla. Nothing but the truth.'

Her own heart rolled over. She wasn't ready for this. She'd known she'd have to face him sometime but still felt too raw.

'You're too late, Theo.' Intrigued, she saw his face turn pale but she couldn't afford sympathy just because he wasn't getting what he wanted. 'I can't do this any longer, be what you want me to be. Why should I settle for less than I want just because it suits you?'

If Theo had looked bad before, now he looked stricken. 'I know—'

'You *don't* know.' She loved him and had been ready to accept second-best, just to be with him. To be an unloved wife. 'You did me a favour, actually, spelling out my real place in your life.'

'I'm sorry, Isla. You don't know how sorry. I didn't mean it the way it came out.'

She shook her head, the terrible pain inside blanketed by resignation. Was there any point in more words? She looked him straight in the eye and said, 'I deserve more. More than you can give me, Theo.'

The bedside chair scraped as he collapsed onto it, head bowed. Isla was stunned to see his hand shake as he tunnelled his fingers through his hair.

He didn't look at her as he took a huge breath, then another. Finally he lifted his head. His terrible, stark expression caught her breath in her throat. He looked to be in pain too.

'You deserve everything good, Isla. So does our child.'

She waited for him to try to persuade her to change her mind. Instead he simply looked at her, as if nothing else mattered.

'I apologise for what I said.' He lifted his hand before she could interrupt. 'I'm not making excuses but I owe you the truth.'

'Go on.'

'What I said was terrible and uncalled for and I truly didn't mean it the way it came out. I'm sorry I hurt you.' Theo looked at his hands. 'I was petrified for Toula.'

Isla nodded. 'I know.'

'But you don't. You assumed I was afraid she'd have a relapse if you mentioned the party, and that was true to some extent. But it was far more.' He paused. 'I feared what would happen if she remembered the truth about that night and told the police she was the one who pushed Costa to his death.'

Isla's breath hissed, her eyes popping wide. She'd wondered, given what Theo had said about Toula's ex being aggressive and wanting her back. 'You *knew* she'd done it?'

'No one knew the truth, not even Toula. She couldn't remember anything. But those stairs were a shortcut to a terrace overlooking the gardens and the guest bedroom wing. Toula's room wasn't there but there'd been some problem with the air conditioning in hers and she used one of the guest rooms to get ready.'

He paused. 'It seemed…possible, but Toula was in no state to relive that night.'

Isla remembered all Theo had gone through, both in prison and afterwards. 'You didn't say anything.'

'How could I? I didn't know for sure and I couldn't push Toula. Even if she recovered her memory and it had been her, what would happen? How could I expect her to face what I'd been through, knowing how fragile she is?'

'Oh, Theo.' Isla recalled him saying he had broad shoulders. She hadn't understood just how deep his protective instincts ran.

'I *did* lash out at you and you didn't deserve it. But you needed to know why.'

'You were afraid Toula might collapse again, or maybe face arrest.'

He nodded, his face grim. 'Exactly. I'm sorry.'

Isla shook her head. She wanted to reach out, smooth

the worry lines from his forehead. But it wouldn't be right, not when she was determined to keep her distance.

'How is she?'

Theo's mouth hitched up at one side. 'Better than I expected. She really is stronger. And she'll need to be.'

Isla's heart sank. 'She was responsible?'

He nodded. 'She's been getting flashes of memory since returning to Athens but wasn't sure if she could believe them. She's gone to the police.'

Isla sat up, heart pounding. 'She's under arrest?'

'She's got bail. The authorities say it was self-defence. Apparently her arms and torso were covered in bruises that night, all documented when she went into care that same night. I knew Costa was a controlling brute but I hadn't known how badly he'd treated her. He was trying to drag her out of the house and she shoved him away. The fall was an accident, but she'll have to face trial.'

Isla pushed the covers aside.

'Isla, what are you doing?'

She leaned over and closed her hand around Theo's. 'I'm so sorry.'

'Not as much as I am.' He breathed deep and turned his hand to clasp hers, his warmth enfolding her. 'Toula will need all the support she can get but I think my stepsister is stronger than I gave her credit for. My one regret is you. I love you, Isla.'

She blinked, watching his mouth, wondering if she'd misheard.

'I've worked out I fell in love with you right at the beginning. That's why I had to send you away, so you weren't tainted by my degradation. I couldn't bear for you to be caught up in that.' His mouth was a grim line that told its own story. 'Then, when I finally had you back and recognised my feelings, I took it slowly, hoping you'd fall in love with me too, only to destroy my chances the other night.'

Isla's heart squeezed, remembering that awful time. 'That was fear talking.'

'It was, but that's no excuse.'

Isla thought of all he'd been through. The trauma, the attempt on his life, the fear not just for himself but for her, his mother and stepsister. The ridiculous work schedule, trying to save his company from the scandal not of his making. His decency in dealing with the old man who saw him as an enemy. His care for Toula and for her.

She could choose to be offended and carry a grudge or she could choose to believe his sincerity.

'What do you see happening next, Theo?'

He squeezed her hand, his smile sad. 'I'll take my lead from you.'

Isla hated seeing him this way, a proud man humbled. He'd made mistakes but with noble intentions.

'What I'd like is for you to hold me. I've missed you so much.'

His eyes rounded and for a moment she saw disbelief on his features. But her Theo wasn't the passive type. He stood, carefully put his arms around her and lifted her off the bed. Seconds later she was cradled in his lap, his heart thudding against her ear, his arms strong but gentle around her.

'You're not the only one who fell in love right at the beginning. I never stopped loving you, even when you sent me away. Even when I tried to hate you.'

'Sh. Don't say it, *glykia mou.*' Glowing golden eyes held hers. 'You really mean it? You love me?'

'I thought it was obvious.'

Theo's laugh was the best sound in the world. Bright and full of joy. She'd never tire of hearing it.

'*S'agapo*, Isla. I love you so much.' Tenderly he kissed her and she felt the magic weave through her body like sparkling ribbons of flame. 'We're going to be absurdly happy.'

He sounded so sure she had to laugh, but beneath the laughter was an equal certainty. Theo was her dream come true. No, better than some dream lover. He was real—flawed, as she was, but honest and loving, and they were made for each other.

EPILOGUE

The scent of meat cooking on the charcoal grill filled the balmy evening. Children's laughter drifted over the hum of nearby conversation.

On the shore stood the home where his mother had been born, the place he and Isla had spent those idyllic first weeks. Now renovated, it was guest accommodation, where Simon, as leader of the dig team, had been based the last few months.

'You always were an incredibly lucky guy, Theo. I'm almost jealous,' Simon said.

Theo looked down at the baby sleeping in his arms and felt a rush of tenderness. Niko's dark hair was like his own but his smile was Isla's. As for his determination, he got that from them both.

Theo grinned. 'I'm not going to argue. I know how blessed I am.'

Who'd have thought, six years ago, when it felt like he carried the weight of the world on his shoulders, that life could be so glorious?

'Life's been good to you too, my friend. I know you're eager to get back to Athens to show off your latest finds. And take up your promotion.'

'Well...' Simon shrugged. 'Perhaps a little. But this place is paradise.'

'It is.' Not because of the scenic beauty or sprawling house he and Isla had built. But because it was *hom*e, his and Isla's. Their retreat from the capital, close enough for commuting if they chose.

They had a perfect view over the silvery olive trees to the blue Aegean Sea where some of tonight's guests had moored sleek yachts.

Theo turned to survey the crowd around the spit roast on the vast terrace. There were archaeologists celebrating the last day of that season's dig. Locals from the village beyond the headland. Friends from Athens and beyond, including Isla's friend Rebecca from the UK. High-heeled sandals and designer dresses mingled with jeans and T-shirts and everywhere there were smiles.

Two women emerged from the crowd. Toula in lemon yellow and Isla, mouth-wateringly lovely in a halter neck dress of flame red. His pulse quickened at the sight. Two little girls, one five and one three, rushed forward.

'Daddy, Daddy!' They ran over and grabbed at his legs. 'Yiaya says you have to come.'

'You're needed to supervise the grill,' Toula added.

'In a moment. First I have to talk with my wife. Maybe you and Simon can keep an eye on it for now.'

Toula raised an eyebrow at his obvious tactic. She and Simon had been going out for eighteen months, through the end of her community service. The court had ruled she'd acted in self-defence and she hadn't been imprisoned. Since then she'd undergone more counselling and almost completed her university degree. She'd also visited Spiro Stavroulis to apologise for Costa's death. To Theo's amazement, she'd forged an unexpected if careful relationship with the old man, who'd been shocked at the revelations about his grandson.

Theo was proud of his stepsister.

'Come on, kids. Come and help Auntie Toula and Simon.' His stepsister shot him a knowing look and herded them away.

Instantly Isla moved closer, stroking the head of their sleeping baby and planting a soft kiss on Theo's mouth.

He sighed. 'That's better.' He shifted his hold on Niko so he had an arm free to wrap around Isla.

'Was something wrong?' Misty blue eyes met his.

'Absolutely not. I was thinking how good life is.'

She grinned and leaned close. 'You've been very understanding about me spending so much time on the dig.'

Theo shook his head. 'You understand when I have to work. Besides, it's your passion.'

She kissed him again, this time adding a tiny nip of teeth. 'Not my only passion, *agapi mou*.'

My love. Were there any better words in the world?

'How long before we can sneak away?' he whispered.

Isla's laugh was like sunshine glittering on the sea. 'Too long. But it will be worth the wait.'

Theo held her close, her and their baby, while his gaze roved over his family and friends. Could life get any better?

He kissed Isla full on the mouth, bending her over his arm, enjoying her surprised gasp, and her rising passion.

It was a fact, he decided. He was the luckiest man in the world.

* * * * *

Swept off your feet by
Reunited by the Greek's Baby?
Then make sure to add these other sensational stories by Annie West to the top of your reading list!

The Innocent's Protector in Paradise
Claiming His Virgin Princess
One Night with Her Forgotten Husband
The Desert King Meets His Match
Reclaiming His Runaway Cinderella

Available now!

COMING NEXT MONTH FROM

HARLEQUIN

PRESENTS

#4089 THE BABY THE DESERT KING MUST CLAIM

by Lynne Graham

When chef Claire is introduced to her elusive employer, she gets the shock of her life! Because the royal that Claire has been working for is Raif, father to the baby Claire's *just* discovered she's carrying!

#4090 A SECRET HEIR TO SECURE HIS THRONE

by Caitlin Crews

Grief-stricken Paris Apollo is intent on getting revenge for his parents' deaths. And he's just discovered a shocking secret: his son! A legitimate heir will mean a triumphant return to power—*if* Madelyn will marry him...

#4091 BOUND BY THE ITALIAN'S "I DO"

A Billion-Dollar Revenge

by Michelle Smart

Billionaire Gianni destroyed Issy's family legacy. Now, it's time for payback by taking down his company! Then Gianni calls her bluff with an outrageous marriage proposal. And Issy must make one last move...by saying *yes*!

#4092 HIS INNOCENT FOR ONE SPANISH NIGHT

Heirs to the Romero Empire

by Carol Marinelli

Alej's desire for photographer Emily is held at bay solely by his belief she's too innocent for someone so cynical. Until one passionate encounter becomes irresistible! The trouble is, now Alej knows exactly how electric they are together...

HPCNMRA0223

#4093 THE GREEK'S FORGOTTEN MARRIAGE

by Maya Blake

Imogen has finally tracked down her missing husband, Zeph. But he has no recollection of their business-deal union! Yet as Zeph slowly pieces his memories together, one thing is for certain: this time, an on-paper marriage won't be enough!

#4094 RETURNING FOR HIS RUTHLESS REVENGE

by Louise Fuller

When self-made Gabriel hires attorney Dove, it's purely business—unfinished business, that is. Years ago, she broke his heart...now he'll force her to face him! Yet their chemistry is undeniable. Will they finally finish what they started?

#4095 RECLAIMED BY HIS BILLION-DOLLAR RING

by Julia James

It's been eight years since Nikos left Calanthe without a goodbye. Now, becoming the Greek's bride is the only way to help her ailing father. Even if it feels like she's walking back into the lion's den...

#4096 ENGAGED TO LONDON'S WILDEST BILLIONAIRE

Behind the Palace Doors...

by Kali Anthony

Lance's debauched reputation is the stuff of tabloid legend. But entertaining thoughts of his attraction to sheltered Sara would be far too reckless. Then she makes him an impassioned plea to help her escape an arranged wedding. His solution? Their own headline-making engagement!

HPCNMRB0223

Get 4 FREE REWARDS!
We'll send you 2 FREE Books plus 2 FREE Mystery Gifts.
DESIRE
BRENDA JACKSON
THE OUTLAW'S CLAIM
DESIRE
Married By Midnight
SHANNON McKENNA
FREE
Value Over
$20
PRESENTS
Unwrapping His New York Innocent
HEIDI RICE
PRESENTS
Forbidden to the Desert Prince
MAISEY YATES
Both the Harlequin® Desire and Harlequin Presents® series feature compelling novels filled with passion, sensuality and intriguing scandals.
YES! Please send me 2 FREE novels from the Harlequin Desire or Harlequin Presents series and my 2 FREE gifts (gifts are worth about $10 retail). After receiving them, if I don't wish to receive any more books, I can return the shipping statement marked "cancel." If I don't cancel, I will receive 6 brand-new Harlequin Presents Larger-Print books every month and be billed just $6.30 each in the U.S. or $6.49 each in Canada, a savings of at least 10% off the cover price, or 6 Harlequin Desire books every month and be billed just $5.05 each in the U.S. or $5.74 each in Canada, a savings of at least 12% off the cover price. It's quite a bargain! Shipping and handling is just 50¢ per book in the U.S. and $1.25 per book in Canada.* I understand that accepting the 2 free books and gifts places me under no obligation to buy anything. I can always return a shipment and cancel at any time by calling the number below. The free books and gifts are mine to keep no matter what I decide.
Choose one: ☐ Harlequin Desire (225/326 HDN GRJ7) ☐ Harlequin Presents Larger-Print (176/376 HDN GRJ7)
Name (please print)
Address
Apt. #
City
State/Province
Zip/Postal Code
Email: Please check this box ☐ if you would like to receive newsletters and promotional emails from Harlequin Enterprises ULC and its affiliates. You can unsubscribe anytime.
Mail to the Harlequin Reader Service:
IN U.S.A.: P.O. Box 1341, Buffalo, NY 14240-8531
IN CANADA: P.O. Box 603, Fort Erie, Ontario L2A 5X3
Want to try 2 free books from another series? Call 1-800-873-8635 or visit www.ReaderService.com.
*Terms and prices subject to change without notice. Prices do not include sales taxes, which will be charged (if applicable) based on your state or country of residence. Canadian residents will be charged applicable taxes. Offer not valid in Quebec. This offer is limited to one order per household. Books received may not be as shown. Not valid for current subscribers to the Harlequin Presents or Harlequin Desire series. All orders subject to approval. Credit or debit balances in a customer's account(s) may be offset by any other outstanding balance owed by or to the customer. Please allow 4 to 6 weeks for delivery. Offer available while quantities last.
Your Privacy—Your information is being collected by Harlequin Enterprises ULC, operating as Harlequin Reader Service. For a complete summary of the information we collect, how we use this information and to whom it is disclosed, please visit our privacy notice located at corporate.harlequin.com/privacy-notice. From time to time we may also exchange your personal information with reputable third parties. If you wish to opt out of this sharing of your personal information, please visit readerservice.com/consumerschoice or call 1-800-873-8635. Notice to California Residents—Under California law, you have specific rights to control and access your data. For more information on these rights and how to exercise them, visit corporate.harlequin.com/california-privacy.
HDHP22R3

November Bundles
Ebook Library
HARLEQUIN PLUS
Read, watch, and play with Harlequin Plus
UNMASKED